A Quiet Night and a Perfect End

A Quiet Night and a Perfect End

short stories by
Denise Roig

Montréal, February '96 —

for Huguette & Robert —

wishing you both nothing but happy endings!

Love,
Denise

NUAGE
EDITIONS

Cover art by Mary Martha Guy.
Cover design by Terry Gallagher/Doowah Design Inc.
Photograph of Denise Roig by Sharon Musgrove.

Acknowledgements
"Tiny Dancer" and "Chinoise" appeared, in slightly different form, in *West/Word*, Spring/Summer 1989. "Boy vs. Gravity" appeared, also in slightly different form and under different title, in *The Urban Wanderers Reader* (Hochelaga Press, 1995).

Thanks in a big way to the best writing group around: Joel Yanofsky, Nancy Lyon, Joe Fiorito, Janet Kask, Pauline Clift, Gord Graham, Janice Hamilton and Brenda Zosky-Proulx. Thanks to my teachers: Patty Cohan in L.A., Rob Allen, Terry Byrnes and Carol Bolt in Montreal. To Robyn Sarah, who read this collection early on and told me to keep going. And to Beauch for endless editing, prodding and patience. Last, and hardly least, thank you, Ariel Tarr, for never once saying, "Mom, you're wasting your time. Where's dinner?"

Published with the assistance of the Canada Council.
Printed and bound in Canada by Les Ateliers Graphiques Marc Veilleux.
Dépôt légal, the National Library of Canada and
la Bibliothèque nationale du Québec.

Canadian Cataloguing in Publication Data

Roig, Denise
    A quiet night and a perfect end

    ISBN 0-921833-40-7

    I. Title.

PS8585.O3955Q84 1995   C813' .54   C95-900887-X
PR9199.3.R64Q84 1995

NuAge Editions, P.O. Box 8, Station E
Montréal, Québec   H2T 3A5

To Rafe and Jackie, my parents,
who opened the door
and to Ray,
who has kept it open

Contents

Tiny Dancer

They missed the city, but not too much or too often. There was a lot to tend to out here: sick sheep and irrigation pipes. And of course there was Berry to watch every second of every day. By this time he was wearing his padded helmet and Fran had lost twenty-five pounds.

The house was too big for them, really. Fran kept nothing but her loom in one of the six bedrooms and Berry had his toys spread out between two. They put his bed in the sunniest. That left one for Ned's computer and stereo equipment and one for them to sleep in. They couldn't stretch themselves far enough to include the sixth bedroom.

It was the least desirable of all the rooms, tight and dark. They'd closed the door and, except for early lapses of memory when Fran and Ned forgot which room was where, it stayed closed.

"How many children do you have?" The real-estate agent asked this three times when she first took them out to see the property. Betty Parson seemed the opposite of "country." She wore maroon eye shadow and lined her lips with dark-red pencil, hoping, Fran supposed, for a sophisticated city look.

"Just the one," Ned said quickly.

"One," Fran said when Betty asked again.

Outside, standing in the muddy drive, looking toward the sheep sheds, the pastel sky spreading over them, she asked again: "How many little ones did you say you have?"

Fran just put up one finger this time. She was tired of the woman and her chatter about the house, the land, the neighbors. Of course they'd take it. They didn't know what else to do in this particular year of their lives. The farm would be a good place for Berry—fresh air, open sky, animals—and it would be a place to store all their heartbroken energy, for a while at least.

Berry spent the night before they moved thrashing around in his sleep. They heard him banging against the wall. And they knew there was nothing to do except try to sleep themselves.

In the morning, their three-year-old son crawled onto Fran's lap and sat there, a soft, little-boy lump. Lately he'd been too restless for love.

"Had a hard night, fighter?" Fran asked into his neck.

Berry pressed his head into her collarbone. "I want to go home," he said.

"Well, we are, honey. To our new home. Today. The one with the animals."

"Home!" insisted Berry and started to cry in that new, wavering way, as if he couldn't control the sounds from his throat.

Ned, standing at the sink rinsing out their breakfast dishes before packing, turned around. Since Berry had gotten sick they were always exchanging looks. *What do you think? Something to worry about? Hmmnn? What? So?* They didn't smile any more when they looked at each other over their son's head. They used to laugh like conspirators when one of the kids did something just too, too cute. There were a lot of things like this, things done once that now seemed as if they'd been done by different people.

Ned clunked one of the coffee mugs against the faucet. "Damn!" he said.

"What?" she asked.

"My favorite mug. I chipped the rim."

"Oh." She couldn't get worked up about the little things any more.

She watched him dry the few bowls and cups and the bad silverware, which they'd kept out until the last morning. Everything else was packed. As he bent down to stick the rinsed-off utensils in the box, she saw again how thick he'd gotten. It wasn't that Ned had gained a tremendous amount of weight. It was the way everything had widened. His neck and jowls had swollen full and the extra width around his waist made him move as if he were carrying more than an extra fifteen pounds. He was only thirty-three.

She, on the other hand, had lost every bit of maternal flesh over the past year. Her breasts had shrunk to preteen size, her collarbone now stuck out even under clothes. She joked about it with Ned. "I'm getting downright concave!" But their laughter had the forced, dark hilarity of two people in a roller-coaster car grinding up its steepest, sharpest bank.

Six months ago, as Berry began bumping into furniture, they decided to move away from all that was known. "We'll have horses!" said Fran, sitting up in bed the night they convinced each other.

"No…sheep!" said Ned. "Little baaa-baaa black sheep!" and he kissed her shoulder under the flannel nightgown.

Fran lifted the nightgown over her head. Lovemaking had come sparsely in the past year, grief and guilt having had their insistent way. And when they'd managed to feel almost all right, almost normal—even rarer, when it was at the same time—they'd used that energy for Berry. That night, pre-farm, they kissed for a long time until Fran whispered, "Let's, okay? Please, okay?"

"There'll be more of that on the farm," Ned told her later.

So they gave up their suburban home in Sunnyvale for forty-five acres of farmland outside Sebastopol. Ned would keep some of his clients, would work from home. "After all, market research can be done from anywhere if you're on the Internet," he told their friends. Fran would, of course, keep weaving. It was her calling and comfort. She'd heard there was a local group of artisans who regularly exhibited together.

And then there was the farm itself. Perhaps they might eventually turn it into something lucrative. Someone had attempted a vineyard on the property years before. The tenants after, the ones just before them, had tried apples. "They were pretty successful, too," Betty told them when they drove up to sign the final papers.

"So what happened?" asked Fran, sensing there was more to the story.

"The man, he was real young, too, had a heart attack. We were all pretty shocked," Betty said, shuffling the papers more than she needed to. This was the official moment, after all.

"So he died here. Is that what you're saying?" Fran asked. She could see the man standing on the top of a ladder picking apples, then clutching his chest and tumbling down, pelted by an avalanche of Golden Delicious.

"Well, in a hospital, where most people die," said Betty, sounding defensive. She wasn't about to jinx the sale at this point. You never knew about people.

Fran noted that Berry was busy with paper and markers across the room. He was at an age where he was curious about dead people. Or rather, he *had* been curious. The illness was taking curiosity with it.

"Did his wife try to keep it up…after?" Fran asked.

Betty widened her purple-shadowed eyes. "Now that I really couldn't tell you. Although it seems I heard she'd already moved out at the time of his attack. Rumor was," she lowered her voice, "she was carrying on with someone else. It broke his heart. Literally, I guess you could say."

Ah, thought Fran, broken hearts, last sad scenes. We really know how to pick a place.

Yet here they were, six months later, making the cavernous farmhouse their own, raising what Ned called their "pilot" flock of sheep. Ever the market researcher.

"City boy," Fran teased.

Those first months she threw herself (gratefully, gratefully) into the painting and sanding, the planting and feeding. Even to the extent of neglecting Berry a little. *He'll survive*, she told herself when guilt whispered at her. The major push was for lightness. And that meant a certain detachment from her son.

She dreamed up little pranks for Ned, like hiding his socks, like reversing the salt and pepper shakers. She tickled the soles of his feet when he propped them up at the end of the day to read *California Farmer*. But one night, while she was doing an imitation of Marlene Deitrich in bed, he said, "Please stop trying so hard."

Within a week, Berry began tripping over his own feet and Fran abandoned all pretense that they were having a good time.

"It could be months; it could be years," Dr. Brenner had said to them at Berry's last appointment in the city. They'd been seeing him now for five years, since Melinda. It was the only time Fran had felt fury toward the large, bland man behind the large bland desk. It was a fury that took in the whole medical profession. Who were they to know the self-determining course of a living thing? A day, two weeks, three years. How could they presume to know? And yet when one's child is known to be dying, one hears such speculations. At times one is even hungry for them.

"What do you think?" Ned asked after the second night of seizures.

"I can't think. Thinking hurts," said Fran.

They were sitting on the edge of the tub in the house's one bathroom. She was spraying disinfectant on Ned's blisters. It seemed as if he'd been breaking in the same pair of work boots for months now.

"It's not as if we don't know the signs," he said. She wished his voice sounded warmer as he said this. She wished he would pull her down to his chest, hide her head there. She would listen to his heart, lose herself in that safe sound. But he was looking at his toes, pulling them apart.

Of course she knew the signs, knew the heartless, precise progression of the disease: listlessness, loss of balance, seizures, coma. With Melinda it had taken almost exactly two years from Dr. Brenner's *This isn't easy to tell you* until the sunny morning in October—a sacrilege, that beautiful weather—when there was nothing left to wait for.

Ned was being so uncooperative tonight. Usually he would murmur something consoling, take her in one of his strong-arm hugs, still somewhat rough after ten years together. But he continued to look at his blisters.

"We can't afford to wait as long as the last time," he finally said.

Was he criticizing the way she'd handled the last time? She'd been so bloody strong. Everyone, including Ned, kept waiting for her to crack. And she hadn't. Until it came time to pick out a dress, toddler 4, for the funeral. They'd sedated her so heavily she slept on and off for three days afterward. She'd wake and cry and then sleep some more.

"To bed," said Ned, and let his feet drop to the floor. He put his arm around her. He must have sensed the distance, however, because when they were in bed, he turned to her and began kissing her with some urgency.

"Let me get my diaphragm," said Fran. There was no margin for error at this point. "Zero population growth," Ned had joked once when they were still joking.

"Not yet," he said, still kissing her.

But she couldn't relax. His lips felt stiff, invasive even. He wasn't giving her time to react. *Slow down.*

"I don't want to get up later," she said and almost had to push him off her to sit up.

That's when they heard the sound of someone singing. It sounded like Berry, but Berry singing like a girl, like Melinda. It was nearly nine-thirty. Fran had tucked him in more than an hour ago. They tried not to run down the hall. The night light—a little clown with a bouquet of lit-up balloons—was still on, but Berry wasn't there.

Further down the hall, they found the door to the closed bedroom open, and inside, glowing like a snowflake in his white sleeper, was Berry, dancing. He swayed, he bounced in his sleeper feet, he twirled. The boy saw them, but kept moving, kept singing in that high voice. Fran couldn't understand the words exactly, but she could tell it was a happy song. They let him go for a long time.

When Berry finally lost his balance, Ned bent to lift him. And as he straightened up, he looked at Fran and she looked at him and something not unlike joy passed between them.

The Real Secret
of Happiness

My father liked three things in life: Louis Armstrong, watering the lawn and burning trash. The rest, he said, was stupid. Stupid was one of his favorite words.

We grew up, my two brothers and I, in a motel on a lake. It was a plain kind of building, white wood with green trim like a thousand other motels you pass on the highway in northern Idaho. But the lake was pretty. Big, too, shaped almost like a heart. You couldn't tell the shape from standing on the edge. You had to see it on a map.

My father did the books. My mother did the rooms. I did the linens because I was the oldest and the only girl. I washed and folded the sheets every Saturday and Sunday afternoon. I learned about life from those sheets, about places other than the lake and about people other than my family. Sometimes I found lipstick stains or blood. Once I even found two snails tied up in the corner of a queen-size flat.

The motel was called "Sleepy Hollow" and it was. It was both really. Except for seven or eight weeks every summer when our circular driveway was filled with station wagons and men calling to each other over the roofs of their cars—"Hey, Hal! Number two's vacant. Remember number two? Ha, ha!" They were big guys with white legs and Bermudas that hung low under bellies that said, "I'm a man. Watch it." Until you looked at their red, plain faces, their sunburned ears, their puffy hands. Then they were just boys come to the lake for a good time.

They came without wives and kids. "For a good fff-fish," they'd tell my father, and then laugh, and elbow him, turning pink with their naughty boyness. "This is the place," my father always said. "You want a good fff-fish, this is it."

They usually arrived late in the afternoon as my mother stood sweating in the kitchen, waiting for the cake to come out of the oven. We ate a cake a night in those years. My brothers could down five, six pieces at once, a dozen if there'd been enough. My mother, who was 5'10" and still had the two-dimensional figure of the Sears Catalog model she'd been in her life before us, would duck and look out the window when she heard tires on the gravel. "It's them," she'd say, and go back to watching the cake—Cherry Angel Food or Double Dutch Chocolate, always some mix—through the square porthole of the oven. It was a small kitchen built for a smaller woman. She was always ducking.

My father would be out front watering the lawn when the station wagons pulled up. He watered slowly, without rush, using his fingers to splay out the water for the pansies that rimmed our yard. He'd be there—in khaki pants and golf cap—barefoot, deep in the lawn. Sometimes the cars bumped each other, the men blasting their horns, bouncing against each other's fenders. "Bernie! Fuck off! Hey, guy!"

And my father would keep watering for a few more minutes, surveying them from the slight incline of the lawn. Then he'd raise his arm, the hose in his hand releasing an arc of water into the grass. It was the farthest he'd go to greet people. The men—one or two that were the ringleaders, usually the largest and loudest—would come up the lawn and shake his free hand.

"Hi, there. I'm Jack. This here's Larry. That's Gil in the Winnebago."

"Right," my father would say to the mass of manhood collected on his lawn.

"Great weather, nice place," someone would say.

"Right," my father would say. And then they'd follow him through the door marked "Office," the service porch where my father kept all the keys.

He hated them. He called them the brainless ones, the zits of the world and worse. I heard him call one a cocksucker once when he thought we kids were watching TV in the other room. I was coming into the kitchen to get a last piece of cake and I heard the word. Cocksucker. It held its own in the kitchen, like someone taking up space, like a person leaning against the kitchen sink. "Sam," my mother warned. "Jeanette," my father warned back. They could use each other's names like weapons.

"Sis knows what I mean anyway, don't you, Sis?" And my father stuck out his foot and put it on mine, a gesture meant to be affectionate. "She doesn't suffer fools any more than I do, do you, Sis?" And I shrugged, took the cake and left. I couldn't bear at fifteen to openly agree with anything either of them said.

"What's to hate?" my mother sometimes asked over dinner when my father was ripping into the lame brains, the armpits, the assholes. "It's not hate," he'd say. "It's more like," he paused, steak in his mouth. "More like repulsion."

"It's rude," my mother insisted. "We need them. We need their business. Try and be nice."

"Nice, nice, nice," my father said. "Nice is stupid." And he went outside and watered the lawn even though he'd already done it earlier that evening. And then later, much later, when we'd all gone to our own rooms, we might hear "What a wonderful world," Satchmo himself taking up residence in the den.

It wasn't really a den. My mother just called it that. It was more like a screened-in porch where my father kept the hi-fi and a pile of old records. There was just one chair in there, a La-Z-Boy in crushed brown velour. My father would lie way back in that chair, waving one hand back and forth like he was conducting. The other hand held a glass. Most of the time I couldn't actually see the glass, but I knew it would be full. Something pale yellow. He didn't sing along with old Louis. He didn't even close his eyes. He just waved his free hand. "What a wonderful world."

The summer I was sixteen, things got bad at the lake. Business had been dropping for a couple of years, but now it went straight downhill. A new resort area was growing up around the southern end. And it was snazzy, with a strip of woodsy-looking condos to rent, and a brand-new Safeway with a takeout deli counter. There was even a dry cleaner that promised your clothes in an hour. At our end of the lake we only had a laundromat where the machines worked some of the time.

There were a lot fewer fat guys in big cars that summer. I didn't mind that, but I wasn't so happy about some of the other things that started happening.

My best friend moved away. Patty and I had known each other practically since we were born, so we were friends out of habit as much as anything. We argued about stupid things like who was going to have the biggest boobs and the biggest wedding. But we always made up. We had to. We were the only two girls the same age in town.

Patty's parents owned a fishing tackle shop half a mile down the road from us. But people weren't so interested in fishing any more, Patty's dad told me. He was a short, round little guy who liked to wink and smile a lot, the opposite of my father, who was tall and skinny and wouldn't have been caught dead winking at anything.

It wasn't a matter of moving the shop down to the other end of the lake where things were happening. "Folks down there, they just want to brawl around in their motorboats," said Patty's dad. But I knew the real reason they had to move. "The rents for shop space are sky-high," Patty's mother told me and Patty in private. "It's no place for us. Not any more."

They moved the first week in July to Boise, where Patty's uncle owned a bait shop. She cried when we said goodbye, her pink glasses steaming up as she hugged me.

On the day Patty left, my mother had put her arm around me, in itself something of a departure. I was washing the dinner dishes, staring out the window into the dark. "People come, people go," she said. "You might as well get used to it now." Then she'd gone back to putting the leftovers away.

For days after Patty left, I felt like a robot: strip beds, sort linen, add bleach, stick in dryer. Now that it was summer and school offered no competition for my time, I was expected to do the linen every day.

Business was down—maybe four of our fifteen rooms were booked during the week, eight or nine on the weekends. It was still a lot of work.

I dragged through July. The weather was ridiculously beautiful. And dry. Not even one afternoon was spoiled by rain. My father spent even more time watering the lawn. He was out there early in the morning, a golf jacket over his pajamas, then again at noon, before supper, after supper.

"They'll drown," my mother said, pointing to the rosebushes my father had planted earlier in the spring. They were new and spindly looking among the older, lusher plants. "Stick to your cakes, Jeanette, why don't you?" said my father.

There was a tension in the house that summer that was edgier than usual. There'd always been this testy, knotty thing between my parents. She was forever trying to civilize him and he was forever flicking ashes on her efforts. Still, there had been mornings when he'd put his hand under her apron while she was making breakfast. "Jeanette, Jeanette." He purred her name with a French accent. I could hear the whispers even with my head deliberately down. And she'd slide away, but look back at him, something alive on her face.

Now it turned nasty. They argued about money at every meal. "I'm worn down by this, completely worn down," my mother said once. "And I'm worn down by you, princess," my father said. They didn't seem to care what we heard any more. They gave up protecting us, left the three of us exposed to all that plagued them. My brothers—Billy was eleven, Roger thirteen at the time—would slink off, turn on the TV and watch nice families where daddies and mommies had their little differences but always giggled, kissed and made up at the end, with an "Oh, honey, I love you."

I folded sheets, towels, pillowcases, washcloths. I wrote to Patty in Boise. I experimented with makeup. I went down to the other end of the lake to swim and be part of a life that seemed to be going somewhere. The perfect weather continued, one shameless, clear-skied day after another. But I couldn't shake my mood. I thought about running away to Boise. I thought about becoming a famous singer or an actress. I even thought one afternoon about walking into the lake and not walking back out.

On a Wednesday night in late July, while we were watching reruns and my father was out in back burning the week's trash, we got a call. A large party would be coming up from Boise on Thursday for four days of fishing. Twelve men. A reunion or something. They each wanted their own room. My father started snapping his fingers when he hung up. "Ladies, ladies, step right up." He and my mother quickly calculated that they would bring in nearly a thousand dollars.

My mother and I spent the whole next day vacuuming and cleaning the rooms since some had gotten stuffy and dusty from no one using them. My mother dug into the carpets with the vacuum. She hummed her favorite song, some stupid thing by Johnny Cash. She called me "Sissy, honey." My father had gone out early to the hardware store for extra keys and to the bank so we'd have enough quarters for the Coke machine.

My brothers even got recruited to wash the ashtrays. Whenever I walked outside to shake my dust cloth, I could hear them yelling at each other in the kitchen. My mother had set them up at the sink with at least fifty ashtrays. "Stupid, you're so stupid," I heard Roger shriek at Billy. And then a big crash of water. They soaked the floor so badly that the linoleum had begun to lift up in places by the time we got back to them.

But by two o'clock everything seemed under control. My father had come back from town with new keys, rolls of quarters, matchbooks, pens, scratch pads and postcards of the lake. With business down, we'd really been letting the little touches go.

I was in one of the rooms lining up pens and postcards on the Formica-topped desk when the first cars pulled into the driveway. I gave the bedspread one last pull and lined up the glasses, sanitized white in their starched paper coverings. And then I realized something was different.

I walked outside. It was as quiet out there as it was inside. Five men stood by the cars. They seemed to be waiting for something. Where was my father? "Hello?" I said to their backs. They all turned around and they all smiled. It was a group smile, the same, identical smile, the kindest, sweetest smile I'd ever seen on any man's face and certainly on five men's faces at once.

"Well, hello there," said one man with dark hair parted on the side. He was in a tan leisure suit with shoes the same color. "You must be Sis," he said. And the two men on both sides of him smiled and nodded. "Hi, there," one said. And the other put out his hand, saying, "Now, don't worry. We're not mind readers like they have in the circus. Your dad told us your name. It's real good to meet you, Sis."

I shook it and then didn't know what to do. "Is my father helping you?" I asked.

"He very kindly offered to move his truck around back so we could have room for all our cars out front here," said the man who'd said hello first. He looked down at me. He was tall, handsome even. "You are so lucky to live in such a beautiful place," he said. "But then I'm sure you know that, Sis."

"My name's not really Sis," I said. "It's Cecilia, but my father never liked it."

"That's a lovely name," the man said. "So tell me, Cecilia, what do you do?"

But my father was calling them from the lawn now, keys dangling from his fingers. "I hope we'll get to visit later," the man said to me before they moved away. And the other four all nodded and smiled at me again. "Thanks so much, Cecilia," one said.

"They're weird," my father said at dinner. Three more cars had pulled in fifteen minutes after the first three. I'd missed their actual arrival, but according to Roger and Billy they were as nice and friendly as the first group. One had given Billy a pack of baseball cards. "I don't know if you collect these, son," he'd said to my brother. "But my two guys do. Have a heck of a lot of fun at it, too."

They'd asked Roger about the best places to fish. "They think I'm an expert," my brother said, looking at my father. My father rolled his eyes. "They asked me if I wanted to go along with them tomorrow," he said, still looking at my father.

"Do what you want," my father said, getting up from the table. Clearly the lawn was calling him. "But you've heard my opinion on these guys." He bent down as if to tell Roger a secret. "Weirdos," he said. "You want to hang around with weirdos..." He shrugged.

We sat there, the four of us, eating the cake of the night—
Chocolate Marble with Fudge Frosting—and heard the pipes under the
house groan as they were once again opened up. "Do you think they're
weird?" I asked my mother.

She seemed distracted, nervous that night. She was eating a
second piece of cake, which she never did. "They're gentlemen," she
said. "Something your father wouldn't know anything about." She gave
my brothers a hard look. "You two could learn something from men
like them."

The whole group, all twelve, gathered early the next morning in
the driveway. I saw them through the kitchen window. They were all
roughly the same age—in their forties, I guessed. And they all looked
roughly the same. Most wore light-colored slacks with pastel knit shirts.
And all had clean, short haircuts, no beards, not even a moustache. "It's
the bible brigade," said my father behind me. "Sis, see what they want. I
can't bear so much sweetness and light this morning."

My friend from the night before began waving as soon as I crossed
the lawn. "Good morning, Cecilia!" he called. He looked delighted to
see me. "Can you believe this weather?" he asked. "I mean, *can* you?"

They all wanted to know if Billy and I would like to spend the day
fishing with them. Roger was already outside, looking important as he
showed two of the men a map. I couldn't go anywhere. I had to stay
behind and wash all the sheets from the night before. We didn't do this
as a matter of policy if people were staying more than one night. But
these men had asked us as a special favor, were in fact paying five dollars
more per room for us to supply fresh linen every day. They'd make up
the beds themselves, they told my mother.

"I can't," I told the man. "I have to work."

"I'm really sorry to hear that," he said. And he did look truly
sorry. "We'll have to do something about that. We will, in fact, do
something about that."

"What's your name?" I asked. And the man put out his hand to
hold mine. He smiled so everything was in that smile. "I'm Matt," he
said.

"Are you guys all in a club?" I asked, but he was already turning
away. Still smiling, but leaving. "Don't work too hard, Cecilia." And he

slid into the driver's seat of one of the cars and eased out the driveway. Billy, who was in the last car, waved as they pulled out. One of the men had given him a baseball cap.

When they came back around four, I was still folding towels. Stacks of linens sat on every flat surface in the living room. Roger and Billy rushed into the kitchen, interrupting each other, falling over each other. My father was in the den with the door closed, supposedly doing paperwork. I could hear him banging around and swearing. He was getting an early start on the night.

"Later," my mother told my brothers when they tried explaining what had happened when Matt and John had nearly caught a trout. "And the boat was rocking, man." Roger's voice was loud. I hadn't heard him sound like that in a long time. He used to be a rowdy, fun little kid, but in the last few years he'd gotten really quiet.

"Later," my mother said. "If you boys want any cake tonight, you'll have to get out of the way."

I folded the last batch of dry sheets and walked down the hill with my plastic basket. At most of the doors, I just handed the men their clean linen. They said, "Thanks a bunch, Cecilia." Or "You sure are thoughtful, Cecilia." One, who told me his name was Tom, showed me a picture of his sixteen-year-old daughter. Her name was Angela, he said. She'd made the honor roll last year, so I expected her to look like a whiz kid or Miss Perfect, but she was just a happy-looking girl. Even like she'd be a bit of a hell-raiser.

Matt came to the door when I got to number eleven. He looked the same as he had earlier in the morning. His hair was all in place. He had a bit of a sunburn line on the bridge of his nose, from sunglasses probably. "Cecilia," he said, "I am so happy to see you." We stood at the open screen door. "So tell me what you do up here. Tell me about your life up here."

"I go to school," I told him. "I'm in tenth grade."

"Uh-huh," he said. "I bet you're a good student, too."

"I'm okay," I said. "There are people a lot smarter than me."

"You know, Cecilia," said Matt and he leaned his head against the door frame. "You know, there are always going to be people who are smarter, richer, more beautiful. That's the way it is in life. Luckily, there's room for all of us. Luckily, there's something that's uniquely ours for us to do while we're here."

"Here?" I asked. Did he mean at the lake?

"On the planet," smiled Matt. "The trick, the real secret of happiness, if you don't mind me getting all philosophical here, is finding out what that thing is."

"Do you know yours?"

He didn't go, "Well, of course," and start telling me how great he was. He didn't say anything right away and I liked that. "Well," he said finally, "I believe I do." Just then one of the other men came to the door to ask Matt if he had any Solarcaine. Phil, in the next room, was starting to get a wicked sunburn, he said. "You don't have to leave," they both said to me. But I did. I had a whole couch-full of bath mats to fold.

The next two days were pretty much like the first. They left early, by six a.m., moving their cars slowly, practically without a sound, out of the driveway onto the highway. I'd never heard such quiet cars. By now it was a foregone conclusion that Roger and Billy would go along, although Matt formally asked my mother each morning. "I know we're being selfish, but can we steal your boys away again? They add so much to the day." She was only too happy to give up her "special boys" as one of the men called them. They were out of her hair, and getting some valuable lessons besides.

My father made himself scarce, staying pretty much indoors when the men were around. He came out to water the lawn while they were out fishing and after they'd gone to bed.

It was quiet at night after the men came back from dinner, usually at the ribs place in town. From my bedroom window I could see five or six of the rooms. The men went back and forth into each other's rooms until about nine, talking quietly. Then the doors would close and the lights would stay on maybe another hour. By ten or ten-thirty, all was dark and even quieter.

"What group do they belong to?" I asked my father on the second night.

"Don't want to know," my father said. "Maybe they're Jehovah's Witnesses. Maybe they're members of the Ku Klux Klan." He was burning trash by the back door, stabbing it down with a stick. Bits of black paper rose up and hit me in the cheeks. "All I know, young lady, is that these guys have temporarily rescued us from financial doom." He poked the pile like it was an animal. "They creep me out, to tell you the truth. But I don't have to like them or mind their business. All I have to do is take their money and give them clean sheets."

Their last morning was cloudy, the first gray day in weeks. "If it starts raining, we'll bring the boys back," Andy and Pete reassured my mother. By now, we knew all their names. "A little rain never hurt anyone," my mother told them, obviously counting on one last day of peace.

By noon it had started sprinkling. By twelve-thirty it was pouring. The caravan pulled back into the driveway just before one o'clock. The boys rushed into the kitchen, flinging wet everywhere. "Boss, it was so boss." Billy was jumping up and down. In spite of the rain, or because of it, the group had caught more fish in four hours than they had in the previous three days. They were already unloading their trunks, taking out white plastic pails full of the day's catch.

"May we?" Matt stuck his head in the kitchen door. He looked damp, but fully intact. He put one of the pails on the doormat. "We'd like you and your family to keep the catch, Jeanette, freeze it up for later maybe." He smiled up at her, his eyes open to her and her predicament. My mother started to say, "Oh, no, really," but then she dropped her head. She shrugged, couldn't look at him. "You're such a blessing, Jeanette," said Matt and stepped out of the way so Tom and John could bring in the other pails.

I went out to help them. The rain was letting up now. "Too bad you had to come back," I said to Matt, who was handing the last pail to John from the trunk.

"Everything," he said, "works out for the best. Now that we've come back early we can have time for our little visit."

Some of the men had already arranged for Billy and Roger to play Monopoly in their room. "You come, too," said Matt.

"The laundry," I said.

"I'll talk to your mom," he said.

My mother relented apparently. How could she say no after the fish? Matt knocked on the kitchen door at three-thirty. He'd put on a new knit shirt. It was pale pink. He smelled nice, like Aqua Velva. He gave me his arm. "Your public awaits you." He grinned. I laughed. We walked—our steps matching—down the driveway, down to number eleven.

I expected at least two Monopoly boards to be out on the bed, my brothers on their bellies, Billy chanting, "Park Place, Park Place." But my brothers were sitting on chairs reading. They looked up. "Hi, Sis," said Roger before going under again. Three of the men were sitting in there—John, Phil and Bart.

"Cecilia," they all said when I came in.

"Well, finally," said Bart.

"She's just been granted three hours of vacation," said Matt and put his arm around me. "And if anyone deserves it, it's this young lady."

It was too quiet, especially considering my brothers were there. Seven people in one room and you could still hear the cicadas outside. "Why is everyone so serious?" I asked. It wasn't a cool thing to say but something didn't feel quite exactly right.

"Oh, there's nothing serious about us," said Phil, leaning back against the headboard of the bed. "We're just regular guys who like to cut up."

"Regular cut-ups," echoed Bart.

They made a place for me on the bed. And then they brought out jumbo bags of potato chips, Fritos, pretzels. Bart went to the other building to buy Cokes. Phil went to get some ice. My brothers kept reading, their hands going in and out, in and out of the bags. They seemed to be reading some kind of comic book.

It was just me and Matt and John. "So tell me, Cecilia, what do you most like doing in life?" It was Matt asking the question and if it had been anyone other than him asking, if he'd been looking at me differently, I would have been able to give an answer that cost me less of myself. I could have said, "I like to read." Or "I like to help my mother make cakes." I could have satisfied them and spared me.

What I said was, "I like to think about things."

"That's my Cecilia," said Matt. "I knew you were a girl who thinks." He paused, reached for a handful of chips. "Like what kinds of things? What kinds of things do you think about, Cecilia?"

I looked over at my brothers. They were gone, dead gone, in those books. "Oh, life," I said. "Love, death, why people are a certain way. You know."

"I do know," said Matt and he looked at me so that I could see who he really was, not just the nice guy fishing with his buddies, but so much more. He was wild and sweet. He was a lost man, a found man. And he was letting me see it all, how he had wrestled and almost lost and then won everything. I never knew a man could be beautiful before, but that's what he was, with his head dropped back, his eyes closed, as if he was on a beach letting the sun soak him through.

The door opened and Phil and Bart came back inside with the ice and Cokes. Matt opened his eyes, looked at the door, looked at me. Bart closed the door behind him. They'd left it open before. "Want a Coke, Sis?" asked Phil.

Matt put out his hand, waved Phil back with a small gesture. "Cecilia, we were all like you once. All of us in this room. Wondering, wandering."

They all nodded and Matt reached his arm toward me. Was he going to hug me? In front of everyone? What if I started to cry? I felt like crying. He reached behind me for the nightstand drawer and pulled out a book. I knew that book. It was my job to dust that book in every room. Usually I forgot.

"It's all in here," said John. They all nodded. They all smiled. "It's so simple, Sis," said Matt.

They left early the next morning, even earlier than the other days. We'd said goodbye the night before. My mother had thrown together a few more cake mixes so she could invite everyone in for dessert before they turned in. "It's been lovely, really lovely having you gentlemen here," she told them. My father had conveniently gone into town to get milk or something.

"Not nearly as nice as it's been for us," said Andy.

"It's been grand," said Tom. "We certainly caught up on our sleep at Sleepy Hollow." Everyone laughed.

"You've got the greatest family, Jeanette," said Matt. "Special, those kids of yours are really special."

"I know," said my mother, but that was all she said about that.

Matt gave me a bookmark that had a poem called "Footprints" on the front. It was about a man walking along a beach thinking he'd gone through all of life's bad times alone. But he really hadn't. There was only one set of footprints because God had carried him when things had gotten out of hand. At least that's what Matt said.

"Sis, don't forget," he said at the door. "You are not alone."

I was sitting on the couch with all the lights on when my father came home that night. My mother and brothers had gone to bed. The lights in the rooms below were all out, too.

"Everybody clear out, Sis?" my father asked. He went into the kitchen, popped a beer, dragged into the den. He rummaged around in there for awhile. I could tell he'd been drinking by the sounds of things hitting each other, things that normally wouldn't come together like that.

"Sis, put out the lights, would you?" he yelled. I went around turning off all the lamps until there was no more light. I sat down, took the bookmark out of my pocket. I couldn't read a word. I put it back. I heard the scrape of the needle dropped without care, mid-song: "And I say to myself, what a wonderful world."

I took the bookmark out again and tore it in half. By the time the song was over, my lap was full of bits of paper. I heard my father's glass fall to the carpet, a soft crash. The needle slid and slurred around and the song started again. "And I say to myself..."

I stood up, the papers spilling. "Turn that stupid thing off, will you?" I shouted. It didn't matter. He was out cold and I was alone. Matt was wrong. And so was Louis.

Paula's Progress

It's the way she moves her mouth when she says certain words in French, like *peur* or *jongleur*. Words that end with a soft, trailing "r." When she says words like that, it makes me want to hit something. Not her, exactly. But something.

French is my language, and Paula, my fiancée, speaks it well, actually extremely well. Yet she approaches it with an earnestness verging on terror. She stands in front of you, her eyes pleading for patience, her dark, small head at a tilt as she tries to hear the French voice inside her. She smiles, nods, says, "*oui, oui, oui.*" She listens hard. She purses her lips, looks heavenward and you find yourself pulling for her, even praying for her. You want it for her. You want it for yourself. Get it right, girl, get it right.

It happened again last night. My sister and brother-in-law had us over for dinner with three other couples, and one of the husbands—a tall, professorial type who looked as if he needed an airing-out—came to me after the dishes had been cleared and said, "She's quite a poet, you know." He was ten years older than me, probably married all that time and veering toward the patronizing.

I was gracious, of course. "She does possess an astonishing eloquence in the language, and it isn't even her own," I told him.

"Oh, but she's made it hers," he said, a bit insistently, clearly the type who likes to debate even when there's agreement.

But I'd seen earlier, as we sat around the table, dipping our fondue forks over and over into the pots of bubbling oil, that he'd been uneasy listening to her. He must have seen the struggle in her eyes, the tension in her mouth, every part of her face saying, "Catch me, catch me. I am about to fall."

Of course, the need for rescue quickly became ludicrous, as Paula sailed by us all, finding the perfect word, the just-right inflection, not needing a cue from anyone.

I still get caught up in it. Sometimes I watch her face, bright and tight, as she tells me about some detail of her day. She pauses, searches the air between us, appears to flail. And I think foolishly, "She's not going to make it."

We're getting married at the end of the summer. Paula has already bought her dress: a long, white T-shirt thing with a lace collar that makes me think of a tablecloth. And she's picked out the music, Couperin and Ravel, with some Jacques Brel at the end. She wants us to say the vows in French. She says she likes the words "*Oui, je le veux*" better than "I do."

But when I think of that particular moment, having to look at her eyes, her mouth, the whole fear of her, I want to say, "No, let's do it in English. Come on, English will do just fine."

We met two years ago when I was married to my first wife. It was a student marriage with bricks and boards for bookcases, spaghetti and sex for dinner. Our families got along. We got along.

It was somewhere in that week before Christmas. Lise, my wife, was up north visiting her family. I had stayed behind to grade exams and attend the obligatory party put on by the chairman of linguistics. Once a year in his elegant Plateau pied-à-terre, he showed off his culinary skills and his art collection so we, his poor plebian teaching assistants, could see what might be ours if we sweated enough and shook the dean's hand enough.

A woman all in black—tights, turtleneck, skirt to mid-thigh—was standing on tiptoe in front of the partly decorated Christmas tree. A straight line of black with a silver star dangling from one hand. A man brought a chair. She stood on it. She leaned out, star in hand, snagged it on the bare, uppermost branch.

The man who'd brought the chair turned away to talk to someone else and in that moment Paula lost her bearings. The black line of her body lurched into an angle where gravity could be the only victor. I watched, interested, vaguely alarmed, as Paula's hand reached for the tree, reached and clutched. For one slapstick, doomed moment, she and the tree danced together. It was a short tree and she was a short person. They did not have far to fall. But the rustle of evergreen, the shattering of many tiny glass balls, the flickering of many tiny lights, quieted us all. Paula lay on top of the tree, the silver star glinting close to her cheek.

There was a rush to help her. Even I, loathe to get involved, took steps toward her. I picked up a bit of the wreckage, red and silver sharp as a razor, so she wouldn't cut herself. No, she was fine, she told everyone. "I have lots of padding," she kept saying, patting her thighs, though I'd already noticed she had very little in the way of extra flesh.

The host, my dear department head, clucked over her for exactly three seconds, then began ticking off his losses. "That ball was from Mother," he said, inspecting a shard on the floor. And when Paula went in search of a broom, I heard him say to another T.A., "Well, that's what you get when you invite people you don't know into your home."

Paula swept the hardwood floor around the now-uprighted tree. Her dark, chin-length hair cut across her face as she bent low to survey the damage. Then she crept away. The party went on. I kept drinking and watching for her return. My black pearl among swine.

I spotted her finally on the balcony. It was minus ten that night and she was on the balcony. No coat. Just those sweet, hapless black limbs all alone. I found my coat in the heap on the bed, found the door to the balcony. I expected her eyes to be red. They weren't. She turned, smiled and shrugged, shivering as I put my coat over her shoulders.

She asked my name. I asked hers. She asked me what time it was. I told her. All this in English. She seemed so English, though nearly everyone else at the party was from the East End.

"You're so lucky to be Québécois," she said suddenly in school-careful French, fever in her face. "I'm from Alberta. I always wanted to be Québécois." I almost corrected her gender/noun agreement, but I stopped because she'd begun to cry, black head down, black elbows on the balcony rail.

I took her home. She made me tea and I told her about my dissertation. And then I took her. I had to. All that was male in me wanted to comfort her. Or conquer her. It was too complicated between us already to tell. She clung. I was the tree. She clung. We hit the earth. We were glass, we were light. It was close to love.

"Teach me French," she said to me at five a.m.

"I'm married," I told her. And then in the dark she haltingly conjugated the verb *se marier.* Her accent, I noted, was lovely, quite lovely.

By the time my wife came back five days later, Paula had registered for an intensive French course at McGill. And I had let myself be run over, won over. I realized I had been buried in the obvious: a dissertation, a marriage, a future scholarly career. I had been going along feeling one pale emotion at a time. A little insecurity, a little lust, a little envy. With Paula I was feeling something, many things, all the time. I had volumes inside me to feel.

I moved into her apartment after a short, bad fight with Lise. "I've met someone else," I told my wife as soon as she came back. I didn't wait for her to take her coat off. She was standing in the hall, holding a green garbage bag filled, I assumed, with Christmas gifts from her family. For us, for me. I saw a woman who was ordinary and who loved me. "I'm in love with someone else," I said.

Lise hit me in both shoulders, hard. She called me *cochon.* I told her that none of this was her fault. That it was just life. "Love is really important," I told her. She cried and called me more names. I shook her a few times, but it didn't help. I moved out that night.

In those first weeks, I worked on my dissertation and Paula worked on her French. She would sit at the kitchen table, headphones on, dictionaries open. "*Jean et Paul vont au cinema,*" I would hear from across the apartment, a sentence unconnected to life as we knew it.

And I would go and kiss my beautiful woman on the back of her beautiful head and she would turn to me a face of such happiness that I had to exit, pointing to the other room, mouthing *travail.* Her eyes followed me. I knew they did.

We had just one point of contention in those first months. *Quelle langue?* As a French Canadian and a linguist, I love my mother tongue. But clearly Paula was at a disadvantage. I'd been speaking English for years, had done two years of graduate study in the States where I'd gained a certain idiomatic facility, an ease of expression, if you will. Six weeks at McGill in French is a wonderful start, I kept reassuring her, but…

She was adamant. She wanted to meet me in the only language worthy of our love. "English is the language of business," she said. "French is for poetry and passion." I remember her speeches. They were the last real conversations we ever had in English.

I have to give her credit—she learned quickly. Within days of beginning her second intensive course, Paula could conjugate the subjunctive, was using vocabulary that seemed advanced even to me. Still, it was hardly a fair match.

"I never formally agreed to this," I finally said to her one night about three months into living together. I had done the cooking as usual. *501 French Verbs* was opened face down next to her plate.

Paula looked up at me and I saw the face I'd begun to realize she didn't just wear when knocking down Christmas trees. A look as if the world might explode in bits in seconds, taking her with it.

"You're not happy," she said and dropped her head. The nape of her neck, where her hair came down in a sculpted "V" was exquisitely white.

"That's not what I'm saying."

She looked up, all doubt and trouble. "Maybe you miss Lise," she said. "Maybe you miss someone you can converse intelligently with in French."

It's just so extreme, I told her, sitting down, taking her hands. I wanted some give and take. Sometimes French, sometimes English. I didn't tell her this exactly, but I did miss our earlier conversations. True, we were speaking French, but it was like the language she condemned, the language of business, the business of: What do you want to eat? What did you do today? What movie should we see? Even in bed, our exchanges had lost their subtlety. Paula simply didn't have enough to work with yet.

What she had she worked well. And her accent was gorgeous. She might, I told her, be one of those rare English Canadians who could cradle the French "r" in her throat instead of stomping it flat.

Yet I'd begun to hold my breath when Paula spoke. And to look away. "Easy, easy," I would coax when her dark eyes conveyed the terror of a woman with a knife in her ribs.

"I can't go easy. It's too hard to go easy."

"Well, try to make it look easier then."

Sometimes Paula cried and I would apologize and she'd beg me to please, please be patient. That she'd catch up with me soon. You don't need to catch up with me, I told her. Really, how could she? I was born speaking French. She was twenty-five and just learning. And then I'd tell her that it was I who needed to catch up with her, emotionally that is. I still admired her ability to cry, feel, carry on.

Early in our first summer, Paula announced that she wanted to go to the north of Quebec, to Chicoutimi, for a full-time French course. She would live with a family, attend classes seven hours a day through the university. The eight-week course would be so good for her.

No, I said. It wouldn't be good for us. What about our summer plans? And besides, I couldn't afford it. "But we have a forever of summers to look forward to," Paula said.

As for the $3,500 tuition, she had it.

I didn't know what to say. We had been living solely on my small salary as a teaching assistant. Paula had worked for a month at a daycare center, but she and the director had parted ways when Paula kept pushing for bilingual instruction. I wouldn't have minded her getting any kind of job to bring in some extra money, but she felt a concentrated push in French for now was a better plan. "Then I'll be able to get a really good job." She said this, I think, nearly every day.

So she had the money. Savings, she said. I was nearly as disturbed by the fact of this money, this secret, as I was by the fact of her leaving.

The night before she left we hardly spoke. I suppose I'd continued to believe she was going to change her mind, to cancel out. Up until that last night when I saw her packing her suitcase, I was waiting for this. She knew where I stood, after all.

She was ardent in bed that night. "*Je t'aime, je t'aime.*" She was like a broken record. I wanted her, but I wanted to get even, too, to let her know this wasn't going to be free. She moved up and down my trunk, climbing to the top. I smacked her buttocks at one point. Her eyes flew open in pure Paula panic, but she didn't protest.

The weather turned glorious after she left. I watched other couples in that particular slow-motion bliss that happens between men and women when summer hits Montreal. She sent cards every day. "Don't be sad," she wrote. "Get out. See people." But the truth was that after six months with Paula I didn't know anybody any more.

I sulked. I stayed in. Summer was being played out in the green streets below. And in the bedrooms above and around me. Through the open windows, I could hear everything I was missing.

She called every Sunday. I'd wanted her to come home at least every other weekend. "But this is part of the course, darling," she said. So she mixed and mingled, perfecting her French, and I wrote the final chapter of my thesis, "The influence of the Inquisition on the French language of 16th-century Belgium." The weather turned from balmy to blasted hot.

She came back at the end of those eight weeks remarking at my paleness. "*Mon pauvre chéri,*" she kept saying as she kissed me. I'd lost weight in her absence. And I noticed that I'd begun to lose my hair, to lose my looks a bit. I'd always been considered above-average looking, the tall, dark, etcetera, type. Lise had found me handsome.

Paula looked different, too. Her hair was longer, her face thinner even than before. I had somehow imagined she'd come home looking as if she'd been on vacation. But she looked drawn, still beautiful to me, but older, tenser.

Her French? I had to be impressed. Her speed had picked up and she didn't seem to be translating in her head any more. She exhibited a new polish, even some beginnings of wit. She was, she told me, reading

Michel Tremblay's first novel. "His use of language is wonderful," she said.

Her second night back we visited friends, colleagues of mine. They were all impressed with Paula's progress. Stunned, I would have to say. The English wife of one assistant professor, who was still struggling in French classes at the Y, couldn't get over it. "I am just so, so jealous," she said at least four times. Everyone was curious about her experience. Paula sat at the head of the table, pretty in a black sundress. She described life in Chicoutimi, what it was like to live with people she didn't know. "*C'était merveilleux*," she told everyone.

I watched more than I listened. She still had that bad habit— that's what I now considered it—of looking lost and on the edge of disaster when she spoke more than two sentences. I watched the others. They laughed at her droll observations, smiled when she described the way the children in the household would bring her a beer every evening. And I saw the way several were pitched forward in their chairs. The dear girl. So fluent, but she might need a hand.

That night in bed, Paula told me how much she loved me. "I need you," she said. And then she conjugated, not in the least bit haltingly, the verb *se marier*.

In the long moment that followed, I found myself waiting to feel something appropriate. Joy, desire. Relief at her return even. I reached for her hand. I reached for her breast. Something was building in my chest, but it did not feel especially gentle. We lay there, waiting for me.

And because I couldn't get at it, because I hoped that whatever I was and wasn't feeling was temporary, because I was so startled by my bitterness, because saying anything other than yes meant facing that bitterness, I said, "Well, let's then."

I'm staying on at UQAM, teaching, doing some postdoctoral work. Paula's enrolled in a special program at l'Université de Montréal and in a year should have a certificate that will prepare her for a degree in translation. "Just perfect in terms of timing a baby," she says.

At the moment, she is planning the wedding. I can hear her in the other room on the phone with the florist. In seamless, pauseless French she asks about the price of roses versus lilies. I can only imagine her face.

What do you do with a woman who thinks you can rescue her, begs you to rescue her, but needs no rescuing? Refuse? Pretend? You lay down your coat—over the puddle, the rushing waters, the gaping moat. Yet when she steps on your coat, grateful, terribly grateful, you somehow feel she is walking on you. You feel the heels of her shoes in your spine.

I am not really necessary. But because Paula wants to believe I am, I put my coat down again and again. "Madame…" Coat in hand, doubt in check, I will soon watch her tremble, cast her eyes around, then glide into home. "*Oui, je le veux,*" she will say.

Chinoise

His hands were the color of walnuts, tanner than any other part of him. They held both ends of the scallion as if they were pinching the edges of a petticoat.

"Like so," he said, looking up at her. "Yes?" he said. "Like so."

She took the scallion from his open hand and steadied herself as if she might be getting ready to do the broad jump. The scallion fled from between her fingers, glanced off the edge of the chopping-block table, landed on the floor.

"Ahh," he said, without smiling. "Case of flying green onion." He bent to pick it up before she could drop to her knees and retrieve it herself. After all, he was being paid. After all, this was only her first class.

He breathed in—somewhat dramatically—and through the white silk of his beautifully fitting shirt she could see a few gray-black chest hairs.

He placed the errant scallion back on the woodblock, but she could see he had already dismissed it and her for the moment. "In Szechuan cooking each flavor, each ingredient must stand on own." He would be more comfortable theorizing for the rest of the lesson. Her clumsiness was a painful reminder of the impossibility of anyone learning anything.

"Do you mind if I sit down now?" Ellen asked him, looking

down on his already nodding head. Mr. Hu nodded to everything she said, so this was no gauge for what he might really be thinking.

She sat on the black metal stool across from him. Phil had insisted on doing the whole kitchen in black and turquoise high-tech. "But it's so unkitcheny," she'd kept telling him, remembering her mother's cheery yellow-and-white Good Housekeeping version, with its crocheted potholders and "Bless this Mess" decorative plate hanging above the stove.

"So," said Mr. Hu, "Pick vegetables each meal, each dish. Must do every day. Not like Canadian do: one shopping one week." He looked disgusted at the thought of all those bags of food consumed over time. "Come," he said suddenly. "Not done."

Reluctantly, Ellen rose. Her feet hurt and she could feel a sinus headache coming on. She looked at the clock on the front panel of the built-in microwave. Eleven. They had a whole hour to go. Damn this idea of Phil's. She was good enough, accomplished enough, without this.

Mr. Hu flexed his tan fingers like a pianist about to begin a Rachmaninoff concerto. "I share with you secret," he told Ellen, slitting his already narrow eyes. A deliberate attempt to make him look all-powerful, all-knowing. And she felt again that awful sense of not being in control of one single thing. A woman in her own kitchen—this *should* be her seat of power. Ellen knocked the scallion off the wood-block again as she moved next to her tiny teacher. He shook his head.

The night before, Phil had brought four Chinese cookbooks to bed with him and laid the books on the extra-firm mattress between them. All had yellow stick-it notes poking from the pages. "Mooshoo pork!" he said to Ellen at some point in his studies and smiled so wildly at her she thought he might be suggesting something else. But no, he just meant mooshoo pork.

After long minutes of listening to him opening and closing books, thumbing indexes, she realized he must be looking for the definitive recipe.

Ellen had been lying on her side reading *Little Women*. "Kind of old for that, aren't you?" Phil asked.

"I just like it," Ellen said. "She still has a lot to say."

"Maybe to your grandmother's generation," said Phil, and went back to his stick-its.

Maybe she was lagging in what was current. But Jo and Beth and Amy and Meg, not to mention their dear old Marmie, still made more sense than reading the ingredients for eighteen varieties of bou. Bou...just the word made her salivate, and not the good kind of salivating.

A month ago, after Phil's open house for new clients, which he'd done as a dim sum party catered by two Chinese restaurants—Mr. Hu, in fact, owned one: Hu's Szechuan Palace—Phil had hit on the idea of giving her Chinese cooking lessons. "Next time, little lady, *you'll* do it." Phil had squeezed her to his side, the way a coach congratulates one of his players for a choice move.

And here they were, the three of them—Mr. Hu, Ellen and Phil—standing in the steely kitchen the morning of the first lesson. Phil was off to a combination tennis game/client meeting.

"Teach her everything you can," Phil called to Mr. Hu as he left the kitchen, his tennis racket raised as if in some international salute.

Immediately Mr. Hu had gone to the sink and begun washing his hands. He'd brought his own soap—a yellow bar wrapped in wax paper. "Here," he said to Ellen, beckoning her to the sink. The soap smelled faintly of fish.

"I'll go wash in the bathroom upstairs," she told him and made for the stairs. She only partly understood why she jerked the faucet handles on and off so roughly, why she stuck her tongue out at her tailored, big-boned, blond self in the mirror. She'd wrapped a full-length white chef's apron over her knit shirt and cords and now looked like a tall sack of flour.

In the kitchen, Mr. Hu waited for her, ballet-size feet joined at the heels, arms at his sides. On the woodblock in front of him—the only thing not chrome or Formica-surfaced in the room—sat a tomato.

"Begin," he said.

Under his fingers the tomato became a rose, with pale, crimson petals peeling out from its ruby center. He flourished the small, serrated knife, performing sleight of hand. Ellen half expected the knife, or the tomato for that matter, to disappear.

Standing this close, she could watch the little man more closely. He could be fifty or sixty. Maybe even seventy. It was so hard to tell with these small-boned Asians and their taut-skinned faces. His eyes had the clouded, yellow look of an old man, but his lips were unlined, full and quite pink. That's when she noticed the eyebrow pencil. She was still staring at the thin line of obviously manufactured brow when he looked up.

"At hands, please," he said and tapped the knife on the chopping board to get her attention. To admonish her. Her eyes had wandered to where they were not welcome.

"Focus, must always focus," he said.

How dare he? Ellen crossed her arms against the white smock of the apron.

Was he gay? A dandy? Who was this spare, humorless, driven little man turning tomatoes into roses in her kitchen and charging her for it? Well, not her. Phil. It was a sad, sore, embarrassing fact to Ellen that she had no money of her own these days. It meant she could argue about nothing.

Mr. Hu next turned a mere orange into a goldfish. Its fins fanned out in impossibly thin slices.

"Next time, soup," he told her half an hour later. He was rubbing his knives with a cloth. "Never water," he said, shaking them toward her. Then he wrapped the yellow soap back in its wax paper and left without saying goodbye.

There would be no next time, of course. Ellen told Phil this as soon as he came home—late; the meeting had run way over as usual. "Just chill, honey, would you?" When she walked away without answering, he called after her, "Hey, you know how those Buddha-heads are!"

But when Mr. Hu called four days later and instructed her to buy four leeks, a head of cabbage, sesame oil and some incense for the next lesson, Ellen didn't tell him not to come.

He showed up at five to nine the next Saturday. She hadn't heard a car pull up in front. And she noticed no unfamiliar cars on the street when opening the door for him. He'd brought a laundry bag this time and set it on the woodblock. Today he was wearing a pale-pink version of the same translucent shirt. And eyebrow pencil. Ellen made sure to check this first thing, when she could look him in the face at the door and not be accused of staring at the wrong things.

"Missus," was all he'd said at the door, bowing his head slightly. Ellen almost corrected him: *Miss.* But she didn't want to confuse him. Or offend him. Theirs were different cultures, after all. It was hard enough explaining it to her own mother, this living together without being married.

Besides, this was going to be Mr. Hu's last stint in her kitchen anyway. It didn't matter that he get the particulars about her and Phil straight. She would let the little Chinese man teach her how to make bird's nest soup this time, then wait a polite day or two and call to cancel the remaining classes. She hoped she wouldn't have to talk to him herself, could just leave the message with the restaurant cashier.

"Incense," Mr. Hu commanded, as he dried his hands on one of her dish towels. Ellen must have looked blank because he glanced up at her from under those sharp little brows and sniffed in sharply several times. "You know," he said, sniffing again. "Incense. You forget to buy?"

Ellen nodded and brought the small paper bag that had been sitting on the counter for the past few days. She hadn't known what kind to buy as she'd wandered through the import store. It had been filled with flowered rattan furniture, all of it lopsided. She was glad she'd outgrown that phase. Phil's high-tech taste was cold, but this was worse. The store was empty, except for two other women, refugees like herself from the real world of work. Kept women, keeping themselves busy in places like this.

In the end, she bought six different kinds of incense—some cones, some sticks.

"Ahh," said Mr. Hu, turning the package on its end so they all rolled out on the counter. "Very good." It was the first time he'd offered encouragement. He plucked one cinnamon-colored cone from the mound, drew a pack of matches from his pocket and lit it. An exotic, tragic smell filled the area where they stood.

This morning Ellen did not watch the clock. There were too many things to tend to—the cabbage simmering on the pot, the rice steaming away next to it. There were snow peas to crack and dried peppers to mince. "Make pieces same size as rice grains," he told her.

When they were done, Mr. Hu drew out two towel-wrapped bundles from his laundry bag. Inside were two rice bowls, unmatched, but intricately, beautifully painted.

"Now taste," he told Ellen.

They sat at the table facing each other. Mr. Hu offered no spoons. Instead he lifted the bowl to his mouth and began pouring it down. Ellen copied him. "No noise," he corrected her. She let the chunky liquid fill her mouth. It meant she had to breathe deeply through her nose. She breathed and swallowed, breathed and swallowed. The soup had a complicated flavor and confusing texture. She liked it.

After he left, Ellen lay down for a long nap, wrapping herself in an afghan on the couch. When Phil came home at seven, he found two bowls of the same soup on the dining-room table. Ellen had set the table with black stoneware and gray linen napkins. Two white camellias floated in a silver bowl in the center. Phil said, "Well, what do you know? That little Chink really is teaching you a thing or two."

He found the soup a little on the salty side, but ate all of it. As he excused himself ten minutes later to make some phone calls, he told Ellen, "Keep trying, babe."

The next week Mr. Hu did not call. By Friday afternoon Ellen began worrying if, in fact, he would come. She'd bought more incense, had practiced the soup two more times—which meant she'd had it for lunch four times during the week. She'd learned how to tilt the bowl back and drink and breathe at the same time. The afternoons after this were quiet; she found herself thinking of very little. When Phil came home on Thursday night at three a.m., she didn't ask why.

On Saturday Mr. Hu was punctual; she needn't have worried. This was the third lesson, the next to the last. "Hello, missus," he said at the door. He'd brought a huge suitcase-shaped basket this time. Again no sign of a car. Had he carried all this on the bus? Surely he could afford a car. Hu's Szechuan Palace seemed to be doing a booming business. There were lines in front noon and night.

Ellen was wearing a pink, silky dress under the white apron this morning. "Color good," Mr. Hu said and nodded once. He was wearing his usual uniform—the thin shirt was pale yellow this time—and, of course, the eyebrow pencil.

Today's lesson was on vegetables. Mr. Hu pronounced them "weegibles." From the wicker suitcase tumbled rounds and spears and odd heads of things, gnarly, rootlike, barely edible-looking. Their colors were of the earth…rusts and unwashed whites.

"Most important lesson," he said to Ellen, who winced at the feel of some as she helped stack the creatures on the counter.

"Today, curry," he said.

"Curry?" she repeated. "But that's Indian."

Mr. Hu looked at her with more patience than usual and bobbed his head a few times. Like the black, lacquered surface of a Chinese box, his hair did not move.

"Wait. See," he said.

Ellen let him show her how to peel the ginger, how to cut it into slippery, golden slivers. She let him show her how to hold the knife just so when shaving the edges of bamboo shoots. Together they carved at the counter, letting the skins drop into the chrome sink.

Halfway through, Mr. Hu lit a stick of incense. By ten-thirty they had filled the other sink with chunks and bits and long sticks of vegetables. "Box," he said and winked at her with both eyes. The suitcase was filled with tins and jars like a chemistry set. For the next half-hour he stood at the sizzling wok pouring in palmfuls and pinches of herbs. He let her watch over his shoulder, but would not let her add any spices herself. "Later," he said, but did not seem displeased that she continued to watch.

By noon, the kitchen smelled like the very best smells ever made, only all mixed together: ginger snaps and buttered popcorn and charcoal-broiled steak. Mr. Hu left without eating this time. It was noon. He bowed to the stove. "For mister," he said.

On the couch, Ellen ate a bowl of the vegetables by herself.

She and Phil ate the vegetables two different nights that week, but when she suggested putting some in his morning omelette on the third day, Phil complained. "Let up, okay?"

On Saturday, Mr. Hu arrrived with three grocery bags. He was quiet this morning, nodding only at the door. In the kitchen he opened his bags. There was pork and rice flour and many stalks of pale-yellow celery. "Last class," he announced, "mooshoo pork."

Ellen almost laughed at this. "I'm glad," she told him. He nodded. They worked together at the sink. He told her very little. She watched his brown-as-nuts fingers and let hers follow. "Yes," he said a few times. Together they tenderized the pork. Together they peeled the celery, rib by yellow rib. Together they floured their hands and flattened the doughy pancakes. Together they watched as the pancakes went from pasty to golden in the hissing-hot pan.

She set the table for two in the dining room, complete with sparkling water and cut flowers. They ate in silence. It was without argument the most delicious thing she'd ever tasted. They each had four. ("More than four, big trouble," warned Mr. Hu.) When it was noon, Mr. Hu simply got up and bowed to her. Yes, it was a bow, Ellen told herself later. It was not a nod. "Good luck," he said.

When Phil came home at an uncharacteristically early six o'clock, beat and gray around the edges, the table had been reset. Ellen served the mooshoo pork.

"Looks like we got our money's worth, huh, hon?" he said, adding that next time she should go just a *little* lighter on the sesame oil.

Finishing her four pancakes, Ellen excused herself and went into the kitchen where she wrapped the leftovers in foil and plastic wrap, labeled the package "Mooshoo pork, June 19," and put it in the freezer. At the doorway she turned off the overhead fluorescents, reached for her purse from the counter, sitting as if it had been waiting for her forever.

At that moment, the pastel outdoor floods—programmed by Phil to go on at dusk—came on, lighting up the chrome palace of her kitchen. They hit the cabinets, the ovens, the perfect floors. She heard Phil's phone voice from the den. Then she was reaching into the dark of the freezer. The package was still warm as she slipped it into her purse.

What The Wife Said
To The Lover

The two women were on the phone late at night. The wife sat in bed, straightening, then releasing, the spiral cord of the phone as she spoke. "It's all different now." She found herself whispering, although *she* had no secrets. The other woman stood in her bare feet, a towel slipping from her waist, listening. They were both his women still, though he now drooled and dropped forks.

He had been a big man, a man always watching his weight. Once he'd said to the other woman, "Chocolate is better than sex, you know." Now his extra flesh had dropped away, leaving big, skin-bulging bones, a rib cage on a grand scale. Even diminished by seventy pounds, he wore an extra-large gown.

They came every day, the women. Discreetly, at different hours. One before breakfast, the other after dinner. "I don't ever, ever want to run into you, do you understand?" the one who was his wife said to the one who was his lover.

They brought their various offerings. His wife carried in week-old copies of *The Wall Street Journal* and recent pictures of their three sons. "Jason, that's Jason," she said, pointing. "He just had his birthday. He's twenty-three, remember? Remember March 20?" And the man looked, then closed his eyes. Against the photos, or against her, it was impossible to say.

The other woman brought expensive hard-bound books: Philip Roth's latest novel, a thick new volume on the American Civil War. He had loved reading history. "This is a new, definitive study," she said right into his face, hitting every syllable like a speech therapist. She read the words on the dust jacket the same way, then placed the book in his hands, against the blanket.

"Bye, my love. Don't forget I love you. I can wait because I love you. Let the love heal you." She always said some variation of this when it was time to leave. Sometimes his eyes tracked her departure; more often they didn't.

After she left, the nurse would pry his fingers from the book and add it to the others on the shelf under the TV. His fingers might stay in that position all night.

They used to make love all night. She was forty-two and he fifty-seven. There was nothing to do except submit to the gift. Discretion, discrimination, these were things for that other life, the one that had hemmed them in with all its lacks and considerations. They bought a piece of land. They talked of a baby. They gave the baby names: Cassandra, Tyler.

Once near the beginning, she'd asked about his wife. They were in bed, still meeting in her apartment. "My wife is a passionate woman," he told her. "But her passion became less and less attractive to me."

She was jarred by this new fact to consider, although he'd wanted her to feel protected by it. "I don't want her any more," he finally said because she'd gotten quiet, seemed to be shrinking under the sheet beside him. "You're who I want. You're all I want." It sounded like lines from songs the man had listened to at night when he was fifteen in his upstairs bedroom, the transistor muted under the pillow.

Travel brochures ("Experience Greece!") lay ready and waiting in the nightstand next to his lover's bed. Phone calls came at dangerous hours ("I had to call. I had to."). The nights with her passed into days, passed into him.

His wife—the tan, the trim, the bright, the really quite wonderful—was finally overturned by the weight of two against one. Their last year together she lived like someone losing her hearing but denying it. She watched his face, she read his lips, she read his mail. It was all wrong somehow. It had gotten all wrong again.

Ten years earlier, when the boys were seventeen, fifteen and thirteen (brutal years), he had moved out. "I can't watch it any more," he tried to explain to her. "All this chaos and ill will." He rented a sparse studio apartment ten minutes away, bought an expensive Abyssinian cat, worked on a long-postponed doctoral thesis, took the boys out for dinner every Friday.

The boys were quiet with him, out of control with her. The oldest brought his girlfriend in to spend nights, the youngest smoked pot in the basement. He, her husband, was sympathetic, but not to be prevailed upon. "Yes, I can see you've got a problem there," he sometimes offered. "Yes, I can see why you'd be upset." He told her she should lay down the law more.

Six months later he was back. He wept in her arms. "I can't believe I was so selfish. I can't believe I thought I could do this."

He brought the cat back with him, although their youngest son was allergic. They resumed their life with a careful courtesy. Sunday mornings he loved her with a close attention to detail; Sunday afternoons he played video games with the boys. It all scared her to death.

They survived nearly eight more years, each holding up their piece of the scenery. The boys went off to college: one, two, three. The middle one, her favorite, got married in his senior year, had a baby a year later. The baby sealed up the last cracks, a beautiful baby.

They bought a piece of land on the coast. He took early retirement and spent the next two years supervising the building of the three-storey house. "My new career," he told their friends.

The month they moved in, he met her, the other woman, at a chiropractic clinic. They compared pains and treatments. She was divorced, a neighbor, a woman without a man, a womanly woman. He went over one afternoon to see how she'd terraced her back yard. They talked for hours. At the door when he left, he said, "I need this."

Their kind of happiness was impossible to hide from the woman who'd known him longer. Even in a house with too many rooms for two people. He moved out, pleading midlife crisis, existential void.

"There's someone else," his wife kept pronouncing, as he kept saying "No, no, that's not it" with a weariness that made her utterly sure. He left behind letters, a stupid oversight. "Teach me to love," she'd written in one. "How I love to come with you," she'd written in another.

The wife went to Spain to seethe, though he was immune by then to her comings, goings, fumings. They, the new they, were building a house. For the second time in two years, he watched as men hammered, sawed and cursed the weather.

But something broke. Not inside his mind—that, maybe they could have fixed—but inside his physical brain. One night as his new love slept beside him, he woke, gagged, vomited and went away.

The lover called the oldest son from the hospital. "Please call your mother," she said.

The wife took a shower before she left the house. The boys were already there.

"Are you his wife?" the doctor asked.

"You could say that," she said. She looked around for the other woman, but didn't know what she looked like.

"She left," the oldest told her.

"We'll need you to sign some papers," a nurse said.

The doctors said he probably wouldn't be coming back. He might, they said, learn to communicate in a limited way. Perhaps his family could teach him sign language. But his body would never feel air all around it again. His legs would never bend or carry weight or wrap themselves around other legs.

They came every day at their appointed times. The lover brought a VCR and rented movies for them to watch. Romantic comedies mostly. Once she brought a nude polaroid of herself. He closed his eyes and moved his hand ever so slightly. She was encouraged.

His wife consulted the nurses about his diet. She opened and closed curtains, rearranged the flowers that still came from their bewildered friends. Once he signalled her with his breathing that he wanted her to come nearer. He rasped something, but she couldn't get it. He repeated it. She shook her head. He dropped his head back, recoiling from her. She nearly slapped him.

When it was time to transfer him to a rehab hospital, the wife made the arrangements. It was not a good sign, this move. There had been some hope while he stayed in the large teaching hospital. Specialists still came in to lift his hands, peer into his eyes. Now the long, unglamorous haul would begin.

The new hospital was a single-storey building smelling of urine and attempts to cover it up. He suffered a setback the first week, aiming the fork at his hair, tugging the catheter from its taped position on the inside of his thigh.

The wife found a photo of him with the other woman, a formal portrait taken in a photographer's studio in brighter times. She dropped it into the trash under his staring eyes.

The weeks passed. She came, she went. She came, she went. One was younger. One was older. One's face was sad with love, the other's angry with it. They never came at the same time.

The older one began to push him. Lift this, hold this. Come on, you can whisper louder than that.

The other woman sat and talked to him. She told him of her lonely life. She held his hand. She kissed him when no one was in the room. Sometimes she looked out the window. Sometimes she cried.

One night she came back. It was late and dark, after visiting hours. She came close to the bed, slipped off her blouse, unhooked her bra, held up her breasts to him in the streetlight from outside. She took off her skirt, hurrying, but when she looked down at him, his eyes were closed. She stood watching his face until she heard voices in the hall, then dressed and left.

"It's all different now."

This is what the wife finally said to the lover, late at night on the phone. Already a box was waiting in his hospital room: books, cards and photos, the VCR on top.

"He's mine. What's left of him," was what the wife finally said.

"I love him," the lover said.

"It doesn't matter," said the wife and stayed on the line, silent, breathing calmly as if she were in meditation, until the lover finally hung up.

The wife stayed away a few days. When she came back, she was brown with sun. She talked to herself. She hummed. She said things like: Eat now. Hold your knife like this. No, like this. Okay, you're getting it.

And then—as she wiped the food from his chin—she said, "You know, it would have been so much better for us all if you'd died."

Boy vs. Gravity

"I don't like this place," he heard the woman say to the man. "There's got to be someplace better. I'm cold, it's cold in here."

They weren't from around there; the boy behind the counter could tell that right away. The two stood across the bar from him. The lights hadn't been turned on yet, too early for that, so it was a little hard to make them out in the tavern's anemic light. It was raining, too, in that steady way of mid-October rain in the Laurentians. The rain outside turned everything gray inside.

He sat down at the bar anyway, the man. Just like that, even after what she'd said. He loosened the wool scarf around his neck, undid the brass buttons on his army surplus jacket, and laid down the thing he'd been holding in both hands, a loose sort of package done up in a plastic bag and rubber band. The woman stood there blinking in the dimness, a clear refusal.

The man ordered a draft. He didn't turn around to check on the woman, just opened his package and pulled out a notebook. It was an old-style school comp book, hard-covered with a marbly pattern in black and white, and full of loose papers and paper clips. He opened it to someplace he seemed to know—the page was already full of writing—and began to write.

He was still writing when the boy brought the beer. The woman was gone. She must have gone somewhere while he'd turned his back to get the beer. The man drank and wrote. He didn't look up, not once. He wrote small, too small, and that was frustrating to the boy. He wanted badly to see what the man was writing. Was it about the tavern? Was it about the woman? It wasn't that he was a big reader. He'd read one book this past summer—*The Firm*, which his mother had lent him. Life had kind of stopped for those nine days. He wasn't a fast reader, at least not in English, but still, he could read. And it was the way this guy was writing, the way nothing else happened for him—not even his disappeared woman—that made the boy behind the counter want to read what the man in front of the counter was writing in his marble book.

The man ordered another beer, looking up in the exchange of glasses. He was what some women would call handsome. Dark hair, dark beard, dark eyes, white teeth. Tall, thin. And somehow barely a man, thought the boy. Barely a member of the masculine clan. Something too fastidious, too conscious—look at that small script—left him somewhere between the two clubs. And neither club would claim him.

The boy had seen his share of men like this up here. They came mainly from the city on little outings, little jaunts. Usually with their families. Men like this needed livelier company—jumpy kids, full-throated wives. Alone together they would fade right into the hillside. Four sissy types (he could see the headline in *La Presse*) went to look at the leaves in Ste. Adele turning green to red to gold and they got lost. Blended right into the landscape.

So he was set against the man. Couldn't help it. It was an actual prejudice, the kind a young man of eighteen might even nourish. It made him feel old, like a citizen of the world, having opinions like this.

Now the woman was back. And the boy felt relieved. Part of him had been waiting for her return. He was curious. But he was responsible, too. His uncle Yves had put him in charge for the weekend. Everyone who entered these doors was his charge. He was in charge.

"It's like England!" she said. She looked ready to cheer. "I swear, Richard, it's exactly like the moors." She said "Richard," but she looked straight at the young man behind the counter. "I am completely won over. And the best part," she climbed onto one of the bar stools, "is that there's a little room in the back with a fireplace!" She *was* cheering and she hadn't let her eyes drop to the man, to the counter, to the man's notebook. "What a dear, dear place," she said to the boy, eyes to eyes. He smiled and turned away, dazzled.

"We're staying," she said and put what she'd been holding, a plastic Le Château bag with black cord handles, on the counter in front of her. Her companion looked up from his notebook, all parts of him elsewhere, then turned back to his writing. "Good," he said to the page.

"Do you serve food here?" she asked the boy and he was forced to speak to her, look at her directly.

"Right here, here's the menu, madame," and he brought out a foggy sheet of plastic under which was a typed menu.

"Look," she said to the man, pointing to the pale, uneven letters. "French f-r-y-e-s."

"*Patates frites*," said the boy.

"Yes, I know," she said, smiling and handing back the menu. "We'll take two specials."

"They're $5.85," he told her. "Five eighty-five *per person*." He wanted to be clear. With English people you always had to be especially clear.

"I know," she said. "Your prices are incredible."

She looked so happy now, sitting there with her leather jacket still on. So relaxed, so at home. She had the kind of looks that were too large for some rooms. Not the tavern, it could handle her with its high-ceilinged blankness and pared-down furniture. She looked closer to forty than thirty, only somewhat younger than his own mother, with a face that was mostly cheekbone, mostly mouth. Her eyes were small and rust-brown, and her hair was nearly exactly the same color. She wore it to the shoulder, curly, with a little barrette on one side. Young-like. He wanted to see her body. You could tell more about a woman from her body than from her face. That's what his uncle said.

He left them at the counter to put in their order. By now she'd pulled out a spiral notebook from the plastic bag and begun to write herself. The cook wasn't in the kitchen. It was four o'clock, usually the time he took a nap to recover from the burger rush at lunchtime and to prepare for the steak crowd at night. Only there were no real crowds at this time of the season and the nap wasn't really a nap, more like a stupor. The cook had a "problem." So the boy left the order—*deux spéciales*, he wrote on a piece of scratch paper—and slipped it under a clip on the empty order wheel.

The man and woman were gone when he came back to the bar. Their packages, too. Not even a tip. He felt the protest rise. They hadn't paid for their drinks yet, come to think of it. He looked around and caught the cocked head of one of the Sunday regulars jerking once, twice, in the direction of the dining room.

He breathed. These were his worst moments, these surprise disappointments in his fellows. He suffered when even strangers did the petty, cheap thing. It was unnecessary, all this meanness in the world. "Run for office," his uncle told him when he complained of the unfairness, of getting stiffed, or getting the butt-end of someone's shitty day. "Either that or get used to it. You got a long, long time ahead of you and most of it, well, let's say some of it's going to be a real let-down."

The man and woman sat at the table closest to the fireplace. Not across from each other, but corner to corner. Both were writing. Only the woman looked up when he came in with two glasses of water. "It's heaven," she said. "If you only knew how much we needed a little nook like this today." And glancing quickly over at her partner, she confided, "We're writers."

"What do you write?" the boy said. He knew it was a personal thing to ask, but she'd already let him in a little.

"Essays," she said. "We both write essays."

Essays? It was a word he was not familiar with in English. Stories. Poems. These were words he knew. "*Comme essayer?*" he asked.

This seemed to amuse her. She bent her head down and looked up, enchantment in her face. "Well, yes," she breathed. "It is very much like that. We try, we try."

He smiled then, too. It was so easy to make her happy.

"Thank you so much," she said to the glass of water.

He left. He would have to find the cook for real now.

They loved the soup. Even the man said something about it. "It's rare to see an establishment bother to make soup any more," he said. "But you cannot equal soup from scratch. What exactly was in this?"

"You mean, what vegetables?" asked the boy.

"Yes, yes," said the man. He could be impatient; now it was obvious. When he wasn't writing, things didn't please him so much. People didn't speak fast enough.

"Cabbage…potato," said the counter boy, now the dining-room boy. He was lying. No one had ever asked this question before. He had no idea what vegetables were in the soup.

"I thought I came upon a piece of celery," said the man. He was wearing black reading glasses, the kind that make the eyebrows go up, that make any question feel like an interrogation.

"Celery, too," said the boy. "I forgot celery."

"We writers," and the woman reached up and held the young man's arm for a moment, "tend to be awfully specific. We love our details."

"Detail is all," said the man and went back to writing. He was on a blank page now.

The fish fillets went down to equal applause. "Light and crunchy," the woman said about the batter. They both cleaned their plates. The woman left the sweet pickle slice on hers, that was all.

But it was the homemade apple pie they raved about. The man got almost excited. "Fresh fruit, not canned," he said at least twice.

"I could nearly smell the apples," said the woman. "I felt like I was in an orchard. *Merci beaucoup*," she said, the first French either of them had spoken.

They wanted tea after. "With milk or lemon?" asked the boy.

"Oh, milk," she said and turned to the man. "Richard, I really do believe we're in England." Richard nodded and tea with milk was served. It was when the boy was bringing a second warm-up pot of water for their teabags that he heard:

"I can't let you do that."

"And why is that, my dear?"

"Because it's my idea, because it was *always* my idea…" And then someone snarled, or hissed, the kind of sound cats make when there is an intruder.

The boy deposited the pot and left, embarrassed and desperate with curiosity. He decided to leave them alone. He'd over-waited them, he decided, there being no other real customers, their being so different, her being so…receptive. He'd leave them be for awhile.

When the boy came back a half-hour later, she was on the floor. Her back was to him; her front to the fireplace. Someone had recently stoked the wood. Red-yellow bits flew into the screen. For the first time he noticed what she was wearing. All of it was brown: boots, sweater, pants. The man, Richard, was not there.

"Hello?" he called from behind her. She didn't move right away, just enough time for a thought, one hideous thought, to fly in and fly out of his mind. Then she sat up; she looked back at him. Her hair was a mess. She said, "I hope you don't mind. I got so comfortable and it's such a lovely fire and it's so rainy out." She looked different from before. Not sure of something.

"It's okay," he said. He came around the front, to the fire, wanting to do something helpful. Wanting also to see the full length of her. He bent down, opened the fire screen and pulled the poker off its hook.

"Don't," she said. "Please don't." He turned to look at her. She was curled on her side, knees bent, head resting on her extended arm. The long brown S of her met him, took him in. "It's so beautiful the way it is," she said. "Don't try to make it better."

He saw that she was a large woman, a woman with an abundance of contour. Large breasts, wide rib cage, generous hips. But all this grandness tapered down to long-girl, thin-girl legs. He imagined her knees. They would indent on both sides. They would be bony. She was the opposite of his mother, who tended to be skimpy on top, ample where her waist ended. I have a following, she would say when she was in a mood to laugh at herself.

"More tea?" he asked, seeing that the notebook was open in front of her on the floor, that a pen was still in her hand.

"You really are a mind reader," she said.

"Your…husband?" he asked.

She didn't correct him, said only, "Oh, I don't know about him."

When he came back with the tea, she was in the same position and still writing. He looked around for a low table to put the pot, cup, spoon, finally placed it on the floor by her notebook. She watched as he poured the water, awkward from this height. She seemed not to be watching the cup, but his fingers. His hand was inches from the cuff of her sweater.

"You've got good hands," she said. "You'll be doing more than this someday. I can tell." He stood up and shrugged, not knowing what she meant exactly. Was she insulting his current job? His uncle had put him in charge. How many eighteen-year-olds are in charge of anything?

But he said nothing because just as he looked down she looked up and he saw for the first time how eyes can say something quite different than the rest of a face.

When he came back an hour later, she was still there on the floor, still writing, still alone in the room. The fire was popping quietly, seething. "Is your husband...?" he asked.

"Oh, he went back," she said.

Back to the city? Back with their car? How was *she* going to get back? It was beginning to make him nervous, all this lying around and writing. The vagueness made him want to sit her up and give her a shake.

"Could you call me a cab?" she asked.

"To Montreal?" he asked.

When he brought her the bill—a grand total of $21.87, two specials, plus two beers for the man, a Pepsi for her—she handed him three ten-dollar bills. "Keep it all," she said. "It was a lovely meal." He tried to read her eyes, but she was looking in her purse for more money. The cab, he'd been told on the phone, would cost close to ninety dollars.

He didn't go back into the room again until it was time to close up. The fire was out now. Only the neon from the service station across the road carried any light into the room. There was her cup on the floor, a napkin, a ripped sugar packet. He picked up the pieces, moved the chairs back into place.

He was looking for something and perhaps because he'd been such an exemplary person all day—waiting on them hand and foot—he found it. Not the marble book, not a card with her name and phone number, not an essay she'd written that afternoon inspired by the day, by his attentiveness, by whatever marital calamity had taken place.

It was one of the pages from the man's marble book, one of the new, loose pages, with a red paper clip stuck in its side that must have pulled free from the others. It was in English and that made it harder to understand. He was hoping for something clear and simple. Something that would explain.

"It's autumn and I have come again to the Laurentians with Ann. On again, on again. We are all fading [fading had been crossed out, dying had been substituted, then fading had been put back]. Why does this trip make me so sad each year? I can feel the cold break into my bones. Where is love, where is romance, where is my soul? Where is the heart of anything? I can't write, I can't think. I can't love any more. It is a brutal burial ground of hope, this season. I am a fallen leaf. I am autumn's fallen fruit..."

The man must have gotten up and left at this point—the paper dropping, unheard to the carpet—or maybe he'd started over or maybe this was meant to be trashed. Because that was the end of it. The boy looked at the page, then squeezed it into a ball. He might not be a big reader, he might have to take English words one by one, but he knew what he liked. John Grisham could write circles around this guy.

But as he washed down the tables, flipped the chairs over on top of the tables, as he counted the cash—all $220 of it, only a so-so day—he felt the downward draw of gravity. It tugged at his ankles, it pulled at his wrists. He felt the weight of a million sad stories.

Reading Conrad

Before she'd even gotten to the end of the first paragraph, a place on the page where the muted afternoon light left a triangle of brightness, she felt a pang of the familiar. She'd spent years reading him, his poems, stories, travel pieces, a novel in all its incarnations. Roberta knew that voice so well. Snarky, she'd once called it.

To read or not to read. She closed the book—a new collection of stories from ex-pat American writers living in Canada…*Defection, Ink*, or some such nonsense. They made collections of everything these days: essays by mothers of transsexuals, poems from disaffected feminist Marxists. The literary world was turning into the Oprah Winfrey Show. She'd found this on a remainders table, where most of those eclectic collections usually ended up. She'd seen his name—Conrad Archer— on the list of contributors and thought, well, hell, maybe it's time.

Roberta slipped in a paper napkin as a marker and looked out the window. It was beginning to snow, the first of the season. Flakes floated and swooped. It was going to be an early winter. Every year it seemed to come earlier.

She got up, book still in hand, and went the ten steps to put the kettle on. Funny how expressions like that endure, she thought: put the kettle on, when what she was really doing was plugging the kettle in. She'd recently conceded to the nineties and bought an electric kettle, kept it on her desk with a sugarbowl—the last, sorry piece from an old set of dishes —which she kept filled with Red Rose tea bags. It seemed something an old lady might do. This pleased her. It also somewhat amused her. And somewhere, it pained her. She waited for the water to heat up—mere seconds—dropped the bag in her mug and went back to her post at the window.

All her life she'd wanted a window seat, some memory of Peter Pan probably. Didn't Wendy sit on a window seat waiting for Mr. Never-Neverland? She'd even told Conrad about her wish for a private nook for reading and writing. For dreaming and doodling, really. Truth was, she hadn't written a word of her own in years.

"I think we can arrange a window seat," Conrad had said, and never mentioned it again. Roberta had finally gotten her window seat eight years ago when she bought this flat, an otherwise unremarkable place in the northern part of the city. The flat's best feature was a bay window in the front, facing the street, which let in plenty of light and which had inspired some earlier owner to build a window seat. The seventies-orange upholstery was going, the stuffing, too, but with a few pillows under and next to her it had become her window on the world.

She opened back to the napkin.

It was the fall of 1962 and Jerry, packed off to college, was thrust into life without father. He lived in a frat house with the other daddy-boys. The place oozed Clearasil, sophomoric discussions about sports and the meaning of life, semen by the vat.

Fifteen years ago, even ten, she would have slammed the book shut. Eighteen years ago she would have ripped pages out. That had been her only weapon when he'd left: I will not read you again. Now she could open to a table of contents, see his name and not scream. Now she could read in calm strides.

Sometimes in the morning walking down the hall to the john he could smell it—the heavy, eggy odor of AWOL hormones, all that dizzy lust shot into institutional sheets.

She closed the pages around the napkin again. Small doses, yes. A paragraph at a time spaced by strong cups of tea to dilute the effect. It was hard to dilute Conrad. His insistent maleness seeped into everything he wrote. She turned the book over to read the blurbs: one from Atwood, one from Ondaatje. Atwood was carefully laudatory: "These former Americans—is there such a thing?—use their words like missiles." And Ondaatje went on in cloudy evocations about writer as explorer. Something about the value of place, south vs. north in the U.S./Canadian sense. What is home? he seemed to be asking.

She turned the book over again to look at the abbreviated list of contributors on the cover, the stars: John Irving, Audrey Thomas, Carol Shields, Conrad Archer. Impressive, very impressive, the company he now kept. And then it was too much; the act of turning the book over consumed the last bit of energy she had for the day. It might be an early night.

"The night opened up to them. And they to the night. All the differences in the physical world were like so much dust."

"Dust?" she asked. "You're sure that's the word you want?" They were lying in bed. The single sheet of paper hovered above them as she read.

It was summer, so hot they were on top of the sheets. "You think I should find another word?" he asked, turning toward her. She could see his dark eyes, so beautiful in this light. This lack of light. "I just think there's another word that's a little less biblical, darling. Less dust to dust and ashes to ashes," she said.

"Yes, Holy Mother," he said, and rolled close so his legs lay parallel to hers. They were all legs. And arms. And sweet, mad optimism. When they woke the next morning, the paper lay creased under her buttocks. "So this is what you really think of my writing," he said, pushing her off.

She'd forgotten her tea. Now it was cool, with a bitterness that nipped her tongue. Roberta took a few sips anyway. Time must have run by her. It was moving faster than she was these days, days that were hurrying her deep into her sixty-sixth year. That would make him fifty, she thought suddenly. She tried to imagine him, almost wished there were photos and bio notes at the back of *Defection, Ink*.

Conrad Archer lives in Nelson, British Columbia, with his wife, the poet Alana Wells, and their three children. He is the author of

Strangers and Fictions, A Bi-Coastal Kind of Thing and a collection of travel essays, *Hither and Yon.* He was once married to Roberta Merrill, the world-renowned reader of others' words. She lives in Montreal with her tea bags.

Pity, the self-reflexive kind, had always, unfortunately, taken her just so far. She placed the mug on the window seat, letting it balance there at a slight tilt. She still liked taking little chances like this. When she was married, she often washed her ring—a Victorian sliver of diamonds and sapphires, Conrad's choice—right over the open drain. What if…the thought used to make her heart thump, her fingers shake, her grip tighten. Wasn't life so damned precarious?

It was years since she'd actually seen Conrad. Montreal, 1987. No, '88. He'd been in town for a few days on behalf of the Writers' Union of Canada. Those had been his words: "on behalf of." Since when had he started talking like an acceptance speech? she'd wondered, hanging up the phone. He had called her, a rare occurrence after the split.

"Hi," he said. "It's me."

"Hi, me," she said. An old game.

A moment followed in which she felt gloriously, unbearably, revived. He must have felt it. "Hmnnn," he said into her held breath. And then he'd gone into his reasons for being in Montreal, paused a moment before asking, "What do you think? Can we do this?" They picked a neutral place, a bar on Crescent below de Maisonneuve, not an old haunt.

It was set for four o'clock, too late for lunch, too early for dinner. There was no choice but to drink. She'd begun before he even arrived: two hasty pints of the dark beer she'd been ordering lately when meeting the occasional student for a conference. She was teaching only one course that year. "Why not let up a bit, Bobbie?" her department head kept coaxing. She was only fifty-nine. She knew what "letting up" meant: We're letting you down, Bobbie, just as gently as we can.

She'd let them down, of course, she the great white female scholarly hope of the seventies. She of the spectacular promise. That's what one editor at the University of Toronto Press had actually said. Spectacular.

She had been trying to make the last inch of her Guinness last when Conrad arrived. He would have been what? Forty-three? Life of the cock and ego, big time. She watched him come into the bar and look around. He'd seen her as soon as his head cleared the door, but he'd paused that extra beat. She still knew his stops and starts, knew the subtle angles of his chin, his bony shoulders. He needed something. That wife of his must be skimping on the admiration, she thought, watching him pretend not to see her yet. Of course, she had bathed him in it. Rubbed love into his shoulders with her nightly massage, spread encouragement on his whole-grain toast every morning, funneled devotion into the pages she edited daily. Years of days.

Conrad saw her, nodded, refused to smile, came toward her. He was limping slightly. She adjusted the collar of her white turtleneck. High neck to cover, white to soften. She'd read something to this effect in a women's magazine recently: cosmetic tricks for the hopelessly over the hill. "I think I'll get a chemical peel," she thought as he reached the table, realizing nearly simultaneously that this was such a cockeyed idea, she must be truly, deeply drunk. Or—worse, far worse—she was still in love with him.

"What's with the limp?" she asked.

"Kids," he said, and eased himself into the booth, next to her but not *too* next to her. She was happy to see him wince. She didn't say anything, just watched as he took off his sunglasses, took off his jean jacket, folded it in half, placed it between them. Separated by denim. She was past denim even then. Vaguely ethnic vests were about all she could get away with. Even the feather earrings had had to go. This was one of the things she especially hated about getting old. What had been hip was now eccentric. What had been sexy was now pathetic.

"I'll tell you, it's great having kids. But it taxes the body," he said, finally, briefly, making eye contact, personal effects now in order. "This year it's touch football."

"How many is it?" she asked. The birth of his first child had nearly done her in: Jamie, a boy who was probably already eight years old. The second birth, a girl whose name she couldn't remember, was only a bit easier to take. She'd heard there was a third child.

"Three. God, they're monsters. God, I love them."

Had he always spoken in this declamatory way? In parallel constructions? Like bad theatre?

"Boy, girl, boy?" she asked.

"Boy, girl, girl," he said. "The youngest is a charmer. She's the one I've been waiting for."

How nice for the other two, she thought. They sat, quiet for a minute, he apparently waiting for someone to come over. She for something to happen. It would.

"You have to go to the bar if you want anything," she finally said. He didn't respond, just kept looking at the bar.

"Really, Mr. Archer. Not everyone knows who you are."

"No need to be testy, dear," he said and smiled a smile so serene, she was thrown, silenced. He took her hand.

"How are you really?" he asked.

The move from cool to warm was confusing. Tears came to her eyes. Confusion, nothing else.

"I heard about you being eased out," he said.

"Who told you that spiteful, vicious lie?" She could sound every bit the windbag as he. Still, she felt a stirring of panic over what he seemed to know. Betrayers; her professional life was rife with them. It must have been Kofax or that new Victorian simp who actually wore black velvet suits when he lectured.

"I was thinking of retiring anyway," she said, reaching for the black wool scarf she'd arrived in—pity it wasn't white —and throwing, twisting, tying it around her throat. The toss over her shoulder felt overdone; she could feel the large movement of her whole arm socket, but she couldn't help it. The small parts of her didn't seem to be working particularly well either.

Conrad looked unconvinced. He took out a cigarette, or rather, he took out a silver case and then took out a cigarette. He's a study, she thought. He's baroque. No, he's rococo. He's a fop. He's...

"I've had it with the pimple brigade anyway," she said.

"Stop pretending, Bobbie," he said, offering her a cigarette.

"I've quit," she said. He looked startled, the first time she'd gotten a rise out of him in so long. "Not the job, stupid. Smoking."

That was a lie. It was just that recently she'd watched herself smoke in the mirror of a bar, seen how the skin around her mouth bunched as she inhaled. She wasn't going to let him see that.

"You've always loved those young minds," he went on. "So much bend in them. Besides, you were in your element in a university classroom. You were one of the best. You were one of the greats."

His repeated use of the word "were" made her decide to knock her glass over. That would bring the bartender fast. A yeasty residue of Guinness pooled at the lip of the glass before it spilled onto the wood. The brown stream seemed headed for Conrad's cigarette case, and after that, his lap.

"Bobbie," warned Conrad. How she loved that tone.

"You called?" she said.

"I believe we've had an accident," Conrad was saying to someone. Roberta looked up, registered somebody tall and male. How had he gotten into this act?

"He used to be my husband," Roberta said to the intruder, who didn't look especially interested in the information.

"I'll clean that up for you folks," he said, and when Roberta focused her eyes again, he was back behind the bar.

"Well, you did. You used to be my husband. Remember?" she demanded of Conrad.

He stubbed out his cigarette.

"I loved you. Remember that?"

Conrad was looking at her with too much sympathy now. She didn't want that, so she stood, leveled her shoulders, steadied herself against the table with both hands. Her lectern.

"He too had bared the front part of his body, and she felt his naked flesh against her as he came into her. For a moment he was still inside her, turgid there, and quivering. Then as he began to move, in the sudden helpless orgasm, there awoke in her new strange thrills rippling inside her..."

How had she remembered this? Every bloody word. Every charged adjective and unexpurgated verb from that master of the word made flesh, her one and only D.H. Lawrence. And she Roberta Merrill, doctor of philosophy—it should have been divinity...she was a divine doctoress—scholar of post-Victorian letters, was here to pay him public homage. Conrad Archer could write his arm off for the next hundred years and never come close.

People seemed to be listening. They were quiet at least. She took a deep breath before plunging back into her memorized (Lawrence seminar, McGill, 1957?) soliloquy: "Rippling, rippling, rippling..." She felt an arm on her right side. Conrad was trying to interfere with her performance. She felt someone on the other side as well. Two people were lifting her, carrying her. Out the door, into the world. Where was the ground? Where were her feet?

His call sometime the next day woke her. "Don't apologize," he said.

She tried to sit up. Someone had forgotten to pull the shade the night before. Daylight pushed her back, flat. There was a question somewhere in her mouth, but she couldn't find it and she knew he would never, ever wait while she searched.

"Bobbie," he began, "You need..."

She hung up before the word. He was the only help that would help. And he was gone.

Roberta leaned closer to the window. Snow could be beautiful, depending on one's mood. Hers she would put at wistful. Full of wist. Was wist a word? It should be. She'd make another cup of tea. That would set her to rights. And a cruise through her unabridged dictionary. Wist. She looked it up: v., p.t. and p.p. of wit, second definition: "speech or writing showing the keen perception and cleverly apt expression of those connections between ideas that awaken amusement and pleasure."

She'd been called witty, she thought, plugging in her magic pot, waiting the necessary seconds for the water to heat, tossing in another tea bag. And she'd been known to stir up amusement and pleasure. Of course, that was in the old days, when booze loosened her tongue and sometimes her clothes. The laugh of the party.

Since she'd stopped drinking last year, she downed tea by the pot-full. The stronger the better. Black tea—hold the milk. Lately, even the sugar. She wanted the taste of the leaves themselves. Of course, Red Rose was no match for rosé. Sobriety, she was told—over and over and over—by the folks in A.A., offered incredible new vistas. So far, sobriety made her feel…sober.

Roberta opened the book back to the napkin. The nice thing about books, the thing that made them different than life, was that you could just close them when you'd had enough. She'd try one more paragraph. One paragraph at a time. Just like the A.A. motto.

Jerry never knew what hit him in that second year at Princeton, his second year at Phi Delta house. He'd been purring along with Bs in Intro to Anthro and getting a piece of sorority ass—tight smiles, tight pelvic floor muscles—just about every weekend.

Tight pelvic floor muscles. Oh, Conrad, where's your editor? He'd always erred on the side of technical exactness, even when it destroyed the sound of a sentence. "You lack poetic integrity," she'd told him, near the end, or was it after the end? The end went on so long. At any rate, it was at a point where she couldn't hurt him any more; he was already with Mimi, the young poet who predated Alana. "He's making Mimi," Roberta told friends. Every time she said this, it made her want to howl with laughter. And other things.

"I lack poetic integrity?" He'd repeated the indictment as a question, rolling the words around with his eyes. Yes, it was after he'd moved out. She remembered now. He was standing in the hall, wearing a wet raincoat. "Well, why shouldn't I lack something?" he'd finally answered. "You lack just about everything else."

"Like what? Like what?" She'd had too much to drink, was, in fact, tanked nightly in those days. There was so much to drink for and with and about.

"Like grace," he said. "Like depth. Like talent." Conrad could sometimes turn a good phrase.

Then Jerry met Ruth Horstman. 'Ich bin Frau Horstman,' she told her students, instructing them patiently in the correct pronunciation of her name. She was a large woman, close to five-ten, with the proportions of a Wagnerian heroine. Jerry was twenty; he put Frau Horstman in her mid-thirties. He had no business being in German III, having jerked off through two years of high-school German. And he had no business bedding her. Even less losing his heart to her.

Damn you, she thought, and felt herself nearly smiling in the snowy light.

"I'll never be much of an academic, will I? That's okay," Conrad had said, not waiting for her to answer, for her to, probably, embarrass them both. "Because I want to write." It was two months into Roberta's most popular undergrad course: The End of Repression: Sex, Love and Politics in the late-Victorian Novel. (Every year she'd fought with the chairman to use titles that would attract students.) The twenty-year-old Conrad was tall, pale, almost handsome. From New Jersey, he said. "The draft," he said.

Six weeks later, over espressos, in the middle of a conversation about Henry James, about the acquiring of style, he said, "I want you."

"Why?" she asked. Those were the days when she could afford to ask questions, to ask: Will this be good for me?

"You're brilliant," said Conrad. "You're beautiful and unpredictable. You're..."

Roberta could see into the young writer's mind. The thesaurus pages flipping furiously: synonyms for desirable, exciting, challenging. She'd been called all these before.

"I could make you happy," said Conrad. "I think I could save you."

And because no man had ever said this to her before, she took him home.

"'He couldn't live without her. She drove him mad with her long, red fingernails and the way she used them down every vertebrae of his back...' I think the singular is vertebra, darling."

"Okay, but what do you think?"

"I want to feel those fingernails. Show me."

"You always say that," said Conrad.

"Only because it's true."

She'd been the mistress of wisdom then, keeper of the secrets of great writing. Now the thought made her snort. What a fraud.

"This, is this better?"

Back and forth, back and forth it went like that. One reading, one listening. Did they ever speak to each other without a piece of paper between them? When his first story—a solid, serviceable piece of short fiction—got published in his senior year, it felt like theirs, *their* story.

He wrote, she taught. There was hardly anyone around them in those early days. Neither family was happy. Hers thought he was too young, a nobody. His thought she was too old, too much a somebody already. "What about children?" his mother kept asking.

What about children? They never got around to that. What about a house? They never got around to that either. What they got around to was his writing.

Foolish woman. She'd forgotten to turn the lamp on. Now she could barely make out the book on her lap. Time really was moving at a clip tonight. Not that Roberta was sorry. She didn't like nights any more. During the day, even the frequently empty ones, she was still a neighbor, a customer, the occasional companion for lunch. During the day she could almost believe she was a fellow to those other humans, the ones out there in the street who were just now coming home by bus and métro from long days away at work. Rush hour, an apt name. The snow tonight seemed to make people walk faster. There was dinner to make, TV to watch, kids' homework to check, husbands and wives to attend to.

"I didn't think you'd mind. Well, not that. I thought you'd understand." The first time he cheated on her he was miserable afterwards, especially when she shocked them both by crying all night and the next day, shocked them both by the depths to which she fell.

"It was just an experiment," he said. "She's a writer. It was material for her novel. There's a girl in it who has an affair. You know, with a married man."

They must have been in the kitchen for that showdown, because whenever Roberta brought it back, she saw herself holding a stick of butter. And there was a glare over them, like the too-bright manufactured light of flourescent tubing. She was always throwing dinner parties in those days: academic colleagues, editors, all manner of literary riffraff. They made good conversation around a table. And, as Conrad said, "Good contacts." By that time, he was looking for a publisher for his first book.

But there was something about the butter. She remembered wanting to squeeze that butter the way she might squeeze someone's pretty neck.

"This girl, is she any good?" Roberta asked.

"It was interesting to be with a different body," Conrad admitted, not looking at her.

"I meant her writing," Roberta said.

She later had her little revenge with a colleague in the department, a man who'd always said it would blow both their minds if ever they… It didn't. He drank too much and came too soon and Conrad had only acted hurt for an afternoon.

"I forgive you," Conrad said. And then he'd handed her the first draft of a new story. He'd written a sex scene in which a young man seduces a young woman. It was the first time she'd wished he'd told more and shown less.

The kettle was blasting out puffs of steam. More hot water coming up. More tea to make and throw away. Roberta tossed the old, cold bag in the garbage, rinsed the mug, unplugged the kettle. To hell with tea; it wasn't strong enough anyway. Back on the window seat, she saw that the crowds had already thinned. Everyone was safe inside now. Only the dry cleaner and the *fruiterie*, the new one run by a Pakistani family who seemed to work around the clock, remained open. Flakes flew into her face. Only the glass saved her.

"Take a vacation, Bobbie," her doctor had told her. "And lay off the booze," he'd added. "It's not going to help you now."

She did go on the wagon for almost a year after Conrad left and she did take part of her sabbatical away, in Edinburgh and Glasgow. She'd been planning to take Conrad as a surprise through Eastern Europe that year. He had his own plans, of course. Mimi and he were heading for Rhodes—this from friends—where they would drink ouzo, listen to bouzouki music, write mediocre poetry and screw each other's brains out—this from her own frantic imagination.

Scotland was, literally, a washout. She hadn't remembered it being so rainy. One weekend, desperate to get away from the damp university libraries, she took a train for Pitlochry, a village dubbed "The Heart of the Highlands." It turned out to be a giant, wet golf course. Silver-haired men with silver-plated golf clubs and silver-haired wives were her companions for three days of the dreariest weather and conversation she could remember. None of the silvery husbands even made so much as a pass at her.

By the second day, she decided she would have to brave the greens herself or go starkers. She squished around the impossibly verdant landscape in her rented shoes, taking lousy aim with her rented clubs. Life had never felt so unredeemable. She had made no progress. She was just a fifty-year-old woman swinging blindly.

Watching the snow gusting with new fury, she wondered what she'd expected back then. He was thirty-five. High from the reviews of his second book, his first novel. He was being hailed coast to coast as Canada's answer to Norman Mailer. Didn't they realize Conrad was every bit as American as Mailer? At the time, Conrad had made a big deal in interviews about giving up his American citizenship. As if that could change who he fundamentally was: a Yank through and through. Even his Canadian nationalism was, at heart, American. He was still his army father's son. Dodging the draft—like he later dodged her—had been a nice little show, a morally correct, not-too-damaging rebellion.

Jerry's flag-waving father was in a fine temper over the turn his son's life had taken. "The towering hausfrau" he called his son's lover (behind his son's back). Jerry argued love; Jerry's father argued logic. Ruth Horstman as a lifetime partner defied the laws of logic. How could Jerry explain to his father that there was almost a duty in his love, that he felt he could do something for her? He was a kid, she an established, respected professional. It defied the laws of logic, but he knew he could give her something she needed. He knew it.

Later Jerry would wonder what would have happened if he hadn't gone back to the frat house that particular Saturday night to do laundry and sneak some food. He'd forgotten about the sorority mixer. The place was packed with girls, girls in every shade of pastel. He had a few beers and when the hi-fi belted out Bobby Vinton doing "Blue Velvet," there she was. Hillary: the perfect girl for 1963—pretty, rich and not too experienced in bed. She let him kiss and feel, promising more, maybe, next time. When he made love to Ruth the next night, she already felt like someone he used to know.

Something was happening on the sidewalk in front of the dry cleaner. Roberta could see people gathering around something lying on the ground. People were crouching and bending. More people came. Someone, a man, took off his coat and laid it down. The snow was falling faster now. People came rushing up; they looked official. Roberta couldn't see an ambulance, but every few seconds a yellow light flashed into the falling snow. A gurney came into view. Two men lifted what now appeared to be a woman onto it. The man who'd given his coat talked to one of the ambulance people. He tucked the coat around the woman's shoulders. And then they all moved out of view, beyond her window frame.

Something on the sidewalk lifted up and billowed in the wind, something clear because Roberta could see the building through it. A woman in a quilted coat bent to pick it up and Roberta realized what it was: a jacket or a skirt encased in flapping plastic. It must have belonged to the woman who'd been taken away. She must have been picking up her dry cleaning. The woman in the coat held the clothes high so they wouldn't drag in the snow. The plastic flew behind her, a light-filled sail. She disappeared into the dry cleaner.

Roberta sat, waiting for more. But it just snowed. The knot of people became regular sidewalk traffic. And then for some reason she wouldn't be able to remember later, Roberta turned to the last page of the story.

Jerry heard about her on the news many years later, about how Ruth had died rescuing one of her children from a fire started in the basement of their home. Neither survived. He was never able to describe to anyone, not to his wife, not to his friends, how learning this changed him. He could have saved her. He knew he could have.

The light was completely gone now. She stared for awhile at the two perspectives: at the storm building momentum half a block away where, just ten minutes before, a crowd had gathered, then at the drifts washing up on the sill half a foot away. She looked at the pink-black sky.

Well, she thought, well.

She got up, plugged in the pot, drew another bag from the old china bowl, plopped it in, waited. The snow lashed at the windows, rattling last summer's screens. She felt...she searched for a less obvious word, but there it was. She felt safe.

Roberta let the tea steep, for just a minute this time. And then she drank it, standing up, looking out. The whole hot cup.

Mothers

"Are you sure you two will be okay?" Deborah bent her head to ask the question. One of the hot rollers on the top of her head wobbled, looked as if it would fall out right there.

"Of course we'll be okay," said Ginger. "We'll be just fine. Won't we, Tia dear?"

Tia smiled and nodded.

They were standing in front of a tall, anonymous door on the third floor of a hotel. Deborah was in pink sweats. Women took so many liberties these days, Ginger thought to herself when her daughter showed up in this get-up two hours before. Of course, she'd said nothing. Deborah was forty-two now, a big grown-up girl with practically no tolerance for a concerned mother's comments on choice of dress. Or husbands.

Deborah put the key in the lock and pushed open the door. Sunlight shot into the dark hallway. "It's bright at least," said Deborah as Ginger stepped into the room, slowly taking it all in. Tia trotted behind, smiling bravely.

Deborah remained standing in the doorway as the two women explored their new surroundings. Ginger ran her fingers over the long, low dresser; Tia wandered into the bathroom and flushed the toilet. Ginger looked at Deborah with raised eyebrows as if to say, *Well, what did you expect? She's a foreigner.*

"Chasing away bad spirits?" Deborah whispered, but Ginger shushed her just as Tia tiptoed out of the bathroom, white vinyl handbag still in hand. Or rather, both hands. Ginger had noticed that Tia clutched her purse in front of her at all times. It made her look like a spaniel sitting up and begging.

There were two queen-sized beds in the room and a view of tennis courts through pale, nylon curtains. Ginger had already set her claim on the bed farthest from the door by laying her blazer at the foot. Tia came to sit on the end of the other—so short, her feet in their white, patent leather sandals dangled a foot above the shag carpet. She smiled up at Deborah, then over at Ginger. Ginger winked back.

"Well," Deborah finally said after standing around a little longer, admiring this and that, "see you both at 5:30." She directed this to Tia, who hadn't moved from her perch.

"Okay," said Tia.

"We'll be fine, dear. Don't worry about us." Ginger was there, steering her to the door. In the hallway, it was so dark Ginger could only make her daughter out by the glint of her wireframe glasses. Why wasn't Deborah wearing her contacts?

"Mother, I really am sorry about this. You're being an awfully good sport," Deborah whispered.

"These things happen," said Ginger, refusing to whisper.

"If we could have found any other solution…" Deborah continued, still whispering.

"We make do," said Ginger. "People make do."

"Another thing," said Deborah, dropping her voice even lower.

"Louder, dear. I can't hear you." Ginger could hear perfectly. But if Deborah was going to prevail on her for one more thing, she was going to have to speak up.

"Mrs. De Leon—Tia—isn't very happy about us getting married by a Unitarian minister. In fact, Julio says she's been crying for weeks about it." Deborah looked at her mother as if hoping she'd take it from there.

"I can't fix things that aren't mine to fix," said Ginger.

Deborah looked as if she were about to cry herself.

"I'll be nice. I'll be very, very nice," said Ginger, cursing the whole damn thing to herself.

"I owe you a lunch," said Deborah, "a long, fabulous lunch at The Peninsula. Or maybe tea at that wonderful little place in Pasadena. How would you like that?"

"You've still got a lot of work to do by the look of things," Ginger said, willing herself not to raise her eyes to Deborah's headgear. One of Deborah's roller pins flew off as she turned and half-ran, half-walked down the hall, but she didn't stop.

"So what do you think about all this, Tia, my dear?" Ginger asked, back inside.

"Very nice?" said Tia, gesturing around the room. Her smile was the same one she'd been wearing since Julio had brought her from the airport this morning. Ginger knew her own cheek and mouth muscles could never have stood the strain of so much oh-everything's-just-fine pleasantness. Especially after all that dashing around. Whose idea was it to take them to Universal Studios? They'd been whisked in and out, barely had time for an iced tea in the over-priced tourist restaurant.

"Mama always wanted to see Hollywood," Julio had told her as they toured the studio's back lots. Ginger knew the excursion—tab picked up by Julio and Deborah—was also her little consolation prize for not making a bigger fuss, for not being the prima donna that she could have been. Some prize. She could go to Universal Studios any time she wanted. She wasn't a tourist in this town. No, they'd just wanted her to keep Tia company, to make her feel at home. When it was she who ended up feeling like the outsider, as they traipsed from place to place. Julio held his mother's hand the whole morning, told her things in Spanish that made Tia laugh. He gushed all over her.

"So what do you think about that, Tia dear? Not enough rooms for the De Leon party?" Ginger began unpacking her suitcase. She pulled out a pair of stockings and walked over to hang them in the closet. "I mean, can you imagine them making a mistake like that?" she asked, adjusting her too-tight curls in the mirror. Why hadn't she gotten the permanent a week earlier? It certainly wouldn't relax by the next morning. She could see Tia behind her.

"No good," said Tia, but kept smiling.

"I mean, I just don't know what's happened to good service in this country," said Ginger. "In my day, this never would have happened. This overbooking business."

"Yes?" said Tia. Ginger had lost Tia now, but kept on about lower standards, no pride in workmanship, the damaging influence of foreign goods.

By now she'd unpacked her suitcase. The only item she'd left in was a gold-framed photo of Deborah and Jack that she took whenever she went away. Under the circumstances it would have been in rude taste. But if she had been alone, if she'd had her own room the way she had assumed she would, it would have been sitting there on the nightstand.

She turned around to get another smile. But Tia had pulled the chenille bedspread over her legs and seemed to be asleep. Was it siesta time? What did Cubans do anyway?

Ginger watched her roommate for a minute. She looked so complete, so content, her beige-stockinged feet crossed and sticking out the end of the covers.

Ginger hung up her last item, the silk shirtwaist she would wear with low pumps for the dinner tonight, then walked to the window. Julio's white convertible was parked directly below.

While she watched, he came out, opened the trunk and took out an overnight bag. Deborah came into view. They stood talking, words she couldn't hear. Julio handed Deborah a garment bag from the trunk. She kissed him on the cheek. He kissed her on the neck. He looked very dark. She looked very light. They continued talking as they disappeared under Ginger into the building.

Ginger lay down on her bed, pulled the bedspread up over her legs as Tia had. It smelled dusty. Didn't they believe in washing anything in these hotels any more besides the sheets and towels?

"Come," said Tia. Her hand was on Ginger's cheek.

"What?" said Ginger, sitting up.

"Eat," said Tia, putting pretend food into her mouth.

"Oh, my God," said Ginger, pulling her dress down. "I overslept. What time is it?"

She stumbled past Tia to look at her travel alarm. It was 5:10.

"Okay," said Tia, behind her.

"No, it's not okay," said Ginger, stamping her foot. "Nothing is okay."

Tia did not move. Whatever her hearing impairment, whatever the limitations of language, she understood. She turned around and began straightening her bed. Ginger saw that Tia's head was covered with many small twists of brown paper, the kind used to wrap packages for mailing.

The sight of Tia from the back made her feel pity and that made her feel angry. Ginger grabbed her makeup bag from the dresser, her dress from the closet and locked herself into the bathroom, not bothering to ask if her companion needed to use it. When she came out at 5:25—breathless, all this rushing around is too much past a certain age—Tia was gone.

Downstairs in the banquet room, Deborah was looking considerably better. Her hair was fluffed and sprayed. She wore a deep-rose silk pantsuit with shoes to match and the dangling diamond earrings her dad had given her the year before he died. Ginger couldn't deny it, she looked happy. Standing next to Julio, swarthy in a white suit and looking awfully young—he was after all, ten whole years younger—Deborah beamed and hugged the arriving guests.

Julio spotted Ginger when she came in. "Ravishing," he told her, holding up both her hands so as to look her over. He was short as men go—five-six, tops—but still towered over her. "Now I know where Deborah gets that flair."

Ginger wasn't about to cave in from the flattery. "Thank you for being so observant," she said, wanting him to know she'd heard such things before.

"And thank you for being so wonderful about the..." He paused. "...the room arrangements."

She just smiled.

"Mama told me how kind and helpful you've been," he said.

Was he being sarcastic? Did he know about her little show of temper back in the room? Or was he simply a good actor?

Julio took her arm in his. "May I?" he asked and walked her over to the long table. Tia was already there.

Ginger almost choked. In fact, she had to cover her mouth and pretend a sneeze or she would have laughed out loud. Tia was wearing a hat. A hat as wide as a sombrero. Red with a black veil, it made Tia's brown little head look the size of a pin. She sat there in a red-flowered dress and a large red hat, a foreigner in a foreign land.

Julio didn't place her right next to "Mama," but across and slightly to the right. "Ladies," he said, and blew them both kisses before returning to Deborah's side.

"Very nice," said Ginger, leaning across the table, gesturing to her own head.

"Nice," said Tia.

"Yes, it is…quite striking," said Ginger, who hated anything except the absolute truth but knew this was not the night for it. And she couldn't very well ignore the hat. Across from her sat a hat.

She didn't have to worry about trying to converse with the lady inside the hat because Julio escorted two of his Cuban friends to that side of the table. Rudy and Cristoban—they introduced themselves to Ginger before sitting on either side of Tia—kept up a steady stream of Spanish through the entire meal. Tia chattered to them. It was enough to give Ginger a headache, all those "ita's" at the end of every damn word.

Ginger's dinner companion to her left didn't help. Flo, Deborah's best friend's mother, was someone Ginger hadn't been sorry to lose contact with when the two girls went their separate ways after college. Flo fretted over Brenda's grades, her reputation (those were the days when such things existed), her marriageability.

"Brenda got a D in Poli Sci," she once sobbed on the phone. Flo had made Ginger feel like a calm, cool mother, like a mother who didn't care too much. That had been refreshing.

Last year, Flo's second husband had died of a stroke. Over dinner, Ginger heard about every detail of his last days. "And then he started spitting up blood," said Flo just as dessert was served.

Ginger managed to get away from the dead man during the rehearsal. Folding chairs had been set up theatre style in a small, adjoining banquet room. The wedding itself would be held in a larger room, but this was the only one available for the run-through. Another tacky touch, thought Ginger.

"All family up front," Julio called. When the two mothers presented themselves—they were the only family, save two cousins of

Julio whom Tia seemed barely to know—he guided them to aisle seats in the first row. "For the Mamas," he said.

Tia still had her hat on. Ginger grazed the side of it when she bent to put her purse on the floor. "*Excusez*," said Ginger, flashing back to high-school French, assuming it was close enough.

"*De nada.*" Tia bobbed.

The others filled in the seats around them. Julio and Deborah walked down the aisle, with Julio and his Cuban friends whistling "Here Comes the Bride." Everyone started laughing at this, except for Ginger and Tia. Out of the corner of her eye, Ginger saw Tia make the sign of the cross.

No one was giving Deborah away. "The only man I'd want to hand me over at this stage of my life would be Jack," Deborah had told her mother the month before, "but I guess that wouldn't look quite right, would it?"

Where was Jack anyway? Ginger sat there watching the handsome backs of her daughter and her second son-in-law. True, they looked good together, even if they were the same height. They even seemed happy together. They stood holding hands in front of the minister (who'd shown up late in cords and tweed jacket, another regrettable detail Ginger had ticked off). Deborah's shoulders were shaking, Julio's head was down and the minister was grinning. "And then the guy says to the priest..." Ginger heard Julio say.

Now Jack had possessed a great sense of humor, but he'd also had a great sense of style and decorum. He'd have ordered prime rib for tomorrow's wedding luncheon, not stuffed Cornish game hen. He'd have been standing a full half-foot taller than Deborah right now. And he'd have made certain that she had her own room.

"Well, I think I'm jealous." Jack had tried to pout when Ginger told him about the impending event. They still got together for lunch a few times a year. Usually she didn't bother telling Deborah. Jack would call and say, "Hey, how about it, beautiful?" And he'd send the car around and whisk her off to some new, must-try place in Santa Monica or Venice or West Hollywood.

"Oh, not because of Deborah, bless her soul. Because of you. Does Julio know that his life is about to be graced with the most elegant and clever mother-in-law in the city? No, make that the country. Ah, heck, darling, the world. Does he know, I mean, does he?"

"Well, what I know is, he's a boy compared to you." Ginger hadn't expected the truth to come bursting out quite like this. She prided herself on being straightforward, but subtle.

"Does he make her happy?" Jack asked.

Ginger didn't like that question. Happiness always seemed to her to be the wrong goal in a marriage. Making an impression, accomplishing something together, now that was a goal. One that Deborah and Jack had achieved with such style in their years together. They'd made each other rich promoting cat food and rock stars and whatever else needed an image boost. Rosetti and Rosetti, Public Relations Consultants.

She thought of her daughter now, still beautiful, still accomplished, and the young man who now accompanied her everywhere.

"We like to be together," Deborah had told her mother, when Ginger wanted to throw a prenuptial party for Deborah's old friends. Minus Julio. "Isn't that why people get married? I love to be with him."

"Well, does he?" asked Jack again. "Does he make her happy?"

"I expect so," Ginger said.

Jack was sipping Diet Coke through a red plastic straw as they waited for a table. "My waistline," he'd told Ginger, patting the torso that hadn't changed in twenty years. Ginger leaned across the bar and pinched the straw, giggled the way only Jack could make her giggle. He slapped her hand.

"Babies this time?" he asked. "These Latins love babies."

Why was he being so serious? Jack was better when he wasn't serious. "Oh, I wouldn't think so," she said. "Deborah's getting up there, you know."

"We're all getting up there, dear," he said and took the hand he'd slapped.

Out of the corner of her eye, Ginger saw Tia dab at her eyes. In between the minister's dry recitation—he wasn't going to give his sermonly all for a mere rehearsal—she heard Tia sniff and sigh.

It was over in twenty minutes. This simple a ceremony didn't even require a rehearsal, Ginger thought, as she collected her jacket and purse.

"Well done," said Julio coming over and hugging her.

"*Gracias*," she said, immediately sorry for the concession. She would not give in.

"Look here, your delightful mother is taking up Spanish," Julio told Deborah when she came over a moment later.

"Be sure and get a good night's sleep, Mother," said Deborah, kissing Ginger on the cheek. "Tomorrow's a big day." It was the way Ginger used to address Deborah not so many years ago. Ginger looked around for Tia, but didn't see her.

She must have left right after the rehearsal because when Ginger let herself into the room ten minutes later, Tia was already in bed. She'd left the muted entryway light on and left the heavier inner curtains open so her roommate could get her bearings.

Across the parking lot were tennis courts lit by rows of powerful stadium lights. A piece of this light shone diagonally across Tia's bed, turning the chenille cover a blinding shade of white. Inside the queen-size expanse lay Tia, curled like a faint bas-relief.

Was she breathing? Ginger moved closer, held her own breath until she saw the rise and fall of something.

She took her time getting ready for bed, put on different creams for different parts of her face. When she came back out, the tennis lights had been turned off. Just a halogen lamp from the parking lot shed a sci-fi glow. Tia had changed positions in the bed, seemed to have buried herself deeper into the center.

Ginger took off her glasses and got into bed. It felt big, bigger than it had this afternoon. She sat up on her elbows for a while, wanting to postpone total submission.

The wedding. Think about that. She'd be wearing her winter-white suit with the pale peach blouse, the softest of crêpes. Deborah would be in her long, white gown. Her groom would be tall and handsome in a black tux.

But she was getting it all mixed up. That was the last wedding. There would be no wonderful Jack tomorrow. Fifteen years ago, when they were all younger and kinder and prettier, there had been a wedding she had been happy about. She remembered the pastel shades of the bridesmaids' gowns, the pearl choker Deborah wore, a special pre-wedding gift from Jack's parents. Deborah had turned many of the details over to her mother and Ginger had run around in a frenzy those last days. There was the five-tiered wedding cake filled with alternating layers of mocha and rum buttercream, Jack's choice. There were the bouquets of pale-peach roses (selected to match the shade of Ginger's blouse) lavished with baby's breath, at every table.

Deborah had never explained the separation to Ginger's satisfaction. Why she'd left that beautiful life with the twin Mercedes, the house in Beverly Hills, the chalet at Lake Arrowhead. Oh, she'd given reasons. So Jack liked to dabble a bit. In secretaries. He decided no kids when he'd originally said he'd consider it. These were things any good marriage could weather. Why couldn't Deborah just go on like a trouper? That's what a good wife was, a trouper.

She wanted to see Jack, right now, wanted to get up and take his picture out of her suitcase. Oh, Jack. What's become of us?

Ginger heard sniffing from Tia's bed. Perhaps she was catching a cold. Maybe she had allergies. The sniffing went on, with little gasps in between.

Ginger lay there, wondering about the etiquette in a situation like this. After a few minutes, she pulled herself out of her bed to lean over Tia's.

"Tia?"

Nada.

"Tia, are you okay?"

Tia began crying for real now. Once Ginger made out a word that sounded like her daughter's name.

Ginger stood in the space between the two beds. The light from outside hit the hem of her nightgown. She lifted the cover on Tia's bed and slipped in. Tia let herself be held and soothed. *"Mi hijo, mi hijo,"* she cried every now and then. Ginger let a few tears of her own run their way down into her hair.

The two mothers didn't take up much more space in the bed than they did separately. Just a little more.

A Quiet Night
and a Perfect End

"Tilt that down, would you, Bunny?" she says and I do as I am told.

Marion's face is in her book, the newest Robert B. Parker. I splurged yesterday when I was in the city. There they were in Barnes & Noble—the whole window full of them, a pyramid of Parkers. I have no interest in mysteries; no stomach either. It's not the violence. It's the suspense that drives me loony. I become impossible to live with when there's suspense going on.

"Thanks, Bun," she says, still not looking at me. I know that until that book is done, she'll be talking in short sentences. She'll be going for shortcuts with meals, too. Pasta with sauce from a jar. Dishes of vanilla ice cream with little wafer cookies stuck in at a rakish angle. Thinking I won't notice.

I tilt the lampshade so the light comes more in my direction. I've got the atlas on my lap, trying to locate a small town in Nova Scotia my neighbor was telling me about earlier today. Damn Rand McNally. They leave so much out.

We have this old lamp, an antique through Marion's family. It's never been all that efficient light-wise, but it sits between our two reading chairs doing the best job it can, which usually means one of us has a bit too much light on the page and the other not enough. I tend to be the ducker, she the squinter. "Bun," she says, "tad less, please."

When the light outside begins to go, around six or so, my wife will get up, sigh dramatically—this doesn't indicate an operatic temperament; it's just her way to punctuate the end of one activity and the beginning of another—and will make her way into the kitchen. Dinner will be simple, as I said. Then we'll head back to our chairs, with a break for the evening news, and we'll read on through till eleven.

I look over at Marion. Not being lost in a novel myself this week, my attention is more skittery. That's the word she used earlier this afternoon. "Shall we go to the library?" she asked. "Find you a good novel to chew on? You're a bit skittery."

She's right. I've felt it all day. From the moment I woke up. Something not quite right. I took an extra vitamin, spent five minutes longer on our Nordic-Trak gizmo. Still.

I let my eyes stay on her. Her beauty is dimming, turning beige where once it was pink. And this surprises me. She was no raving, knockout wonder woman when we were young. Gentle-looking, like a mother deer. When I first saw her and heard her speak, I thought of Bambi's mother. And foolish me, I thought, well, so much for that. I'm not about to jump the bones of Bambi's mother.

I bring myself back to the map, let my eyes run over Cape Breton Island—next summer perhaps, if our collective health holds—and exhale into the deep-breathing my physiotherapist keeps urging me to do. "You've got some old, old knots in there, Ben," she says as she kneads my left shoulder once a week. "Breathe into it," she tells me when I clench and retreat under her touch. I breathe now—in-two-three, out-two-three—and turn my eyes back on Marion.

There's something to do with her, something in this funny day where I feel I'm forgetting a fact or willing it away or...Damn Rand McNally, I still can't find this town. For the next half hour, I lose myself in the Nova Scotia coastline, with a detour to Prince Edward Island. It's been years since Marion and I were there. Next summer, after Cape Breton, if we have enough money, if Marion's feeling up to it...

She's up and bending in close to me. Her book is shut around one finger, her bookmark. Her lips are smiling more than her eyes. "Plotting our next great escape?" she asks and kisses me, harder than I expect, below my left eye, then straightens—without much pep, I notice—and goes to the kitchen.

"How does P.E.I. in August sound?" I have to shout over the sound of the radio, which she always turns on as soon as she sets foot in the kitchen.

"Rainy!" she shouts back.

She's right. Good friends of ours planned two weeks on P.E.I. last summer and bailed—literally—after five days. "Rain and mud, lobster and potatoes. I need more than that on a vacation," Ginny, the wife, had said. They were relieved to get to Bar Harbor for the second week. "Back to the good old U.S. of A.," Lou, the husband, had said. "Those Canucks have a nice country and all, but it's boring. I'll take Western Mass. any day."

I love Granby, Massachusetts, and our old fixer-upper that's perpetually in need of fixing and never stays long on the up. Marion calls this place "the sponge." I'm attached to my routines: tutoring kids at the local elementary in math, helping out at the occasional fund-raiser for St. Mary's Church (no bingo, thank you), going to the theatre in Springfield. But today I'd like to be somewhere else. I'd like to be heading out.

"What about Newfoundland?" I ask Marion over dinner. I was right: it's pasta with spaghetti sauce from a jar. At least she grated the Parmesan fresh.

"Now that's an idea," she says, and I realize this is the first time today she's sounded pleased or eager about anything. I'd put her mood at flat, at three on a scale of one to ten. So...I am not the only one feeling out of it. But I'm more sad than slow. And too irritable for plain old melancholy. Quiet, it's very quiet, this thing sitting on the edge of sight.

Marion begins to clear the table—my, we're both on automatic tonight—and I protest, touch her on the hip, nudge her toward where she really wants to go and what she really wants to do. "Back to your book!" I command. "I've got nothing chewy to read, remember? I wash, you read." She beams as she always does when she thinks I'm a wizard of intuition.

"You're so advanced for a man," she says and leaves me for her beloved Parker.

There aren't many dishes. I stack the silverware in the dishwasher along with the plates—we only dirtied two—wash the pot, the saucepan. I'm about to frost two bowls in the freezer for ice cream later, when I look up at the clock and that's when we collide, me and what's been waiting.

It comes in layers. Shock, first. How could I have looked at the calendar at least three times today and missed it? Then I'm surprised that the hour more than the day triggered the memory. Then bafflement. Marion has said nothing. Has she forgotten, as well? She's never missed the passing of this day. I'm working myself into a fine mental state, weighing and wondering and speculating, because even though I now know what this weird, wearing day has been about, I still don't really want to know.

The saddest day of our life Marion called it. Do you think we'll ever get over this? she had asked then. Oh, I don't think so, I'd said. I knew it was cruel to say that. And I knew it was going to be true.

We decided not to tell anyone, not right away. Marion wanted to wait the full three months, but I knew I'd never make it that long. "I'm too excited," I kept telling her.

"That's how this whole funny business began," she said.

That night six weeks before, her body had opened and I had leaped into the beyond. We were forty and in our fifteenth year of a marriage that was warm and hot in turns. We were getting better at it, I felt. Better at plumbing each other's recesses, better at negotiating the intimate terrain of a relationship no longer new. The love would hold out.

But no children. We'd tried it all by then, the early-morning thermometers stuck in before Marion could even get up to pee, iodine injections X-rayed through her fallopian tubes. For my part, *from* my part, I had ejaculated into plastic tubes, fingering Marion's large and lustrous nipples to trigger a hasty release. Once we stood in a hospital bathroom and Marion stroked me until I slumped against the wall.

By the tenth year, we'd exhausted every bit of medical knowledge and each other. Tired of looking at babies, tired of wanting babies. We went back into our marriage not ungratefully. Marion produced a dozen new paintings that first year, a rush of new vision. I took a sabbatical from teaching and wrote the textbook that had been rattling around my skull for years. We weren't in bad shape; there was a hush on things, that's all.

Then this. She'd felt different from the very first week. "No, really, Bun," she kept telling me. "There's a funny sensation in my head and I think my stomach has moved up to my throat." There were strange tugs in her pelvis. I was embarrassed later at how skeptical I'd been. The first test came back positive. The doctor did another, just to be sure.

"It could be early menopause," he said.

"Screw that," said Marion.

The next morning I was bringing her crackers in bed. By that evening I was feeling nauseous myself, the beginning of three months of mutual indigestion.

Dumpy. Even Marion would call her body that. She's short with no definitive waist (those are my words; she calls herself "The Waistland"). Her breasts? Ah, another thing. I will only say that each more than fills both my hands, and that the sight of those breasts has brought us many, many times into the blissful pocket of our bed.

Pregnancy, however, made her breasts almost impossible to touch. "Are they bruised?" she asked often, looking down at herself. They *feel* bruised." And almost impossible to resist. I wanted to suckle at all hours. Put me to the breast; I shall not want again. "This baby is turning you into a baby," Marion said.

Two and a half months into this brave new life of ours, she developed a craving for fresh air. It must have been late April, the end of a particularly frigid winter. Marion stood at the window, the one in the dining room facing the hills, stroking her belly. She was just beginning to show; the curve that looked soft, but felt hard, raised the hem of her white oxford shirt an inch.

We left at eleven with a grocery bag packed with cold cuts and cold beers. Just minutes on the road and Marion was already fishing around for crackers.

"Baby bile," she said.

"Like hell," I told her. "You just can't wait to eat." It's true: turn on the ignition and Marion's appetite revs, too. Within blocks of the house, she's ready to stop for lunch.

It was a gorgeous, blowy kind of day. Still too cold to take our windbreakers off. At one point, after stopping at an outdoor stand for asparagus—Marion having her mind on food again—she took off her gloves and threw them out the car window. "So long, suckers!" she yelled as they flew behind us. That was the kind of day it was.

We stopped to eat at noon, an hour too early for me, an hour too late for Marion, who threatened to eat the asparagus raw if we didn't stop. I wasn't even sure where we were at that point. Marion was convinced we were just minutes from Worcester and her old alma mater. "I know that hill," she kept insisting.

We looked for a place to toss a blanket. Everything seemed fenced off. And the air was on the cool side. "Our teeth will be chattering so much we won't be able to eat," hinted Marion. Eating was, after all, the point. We landed finally at a pub filled with students, although it wasn't Worcester proper. Marion ordered a burger, large fries and a beer. I picked at a club sandwich, distracted by the loud music and the rest of the crowd. "They're half our age," I yelled over Donna Summer. It was the summer of disco.

"Get used to the young crowd, Bun," said Marion and pushed her dill pickle into my mouth. "I'm in with the in crowd," she sang, then ordered a piece of apple pie over my protestations about the quality of restaurant pie.

We found an antique store in that sort-of town, scrounged among the ruins for awhile. Marion found an old off-white christening gown and bargained the owner down to $8 from $15. It looked minute, too small for a doll even. The woman wrapped it in old Christmas paper for us; she was out of bags. "All the best," she said.

We got lost on the way home, not difficult since we still weren't sure where we were: my fault. I have maps for Italy, for Puerto Rico, for every Canadian province. But local maps? I always assume I can navigate my own turf. We stopped for ice cream sundaes on the way home, at a roadside Tastee Freeze. Marion ordered something disgusting with marshmallow and strawberry and fudge. "This counts as dinner," she said.

Of course, it didn't. By the time we arrived home with the setting sun, she had to go into the kitchen and fix something, "a nutritious snack after all the crap I've downed." We took our plates of salad out onto the screened-in back porch, stood watching the sky as we ate, and when the sky was completely dark, we turned our eyes on each other.

There are nights in a long life with one person that you can recall almost exactly. I remember what her heels felt like pressing into my calves, the way her eyes moved under her eyelids, the way she sucked my baby finger until all my fingers, all of me, was tingling. I remember the slow, swollen wonder of loving Marion on that particular night.

Ten days later she called me at school. "I seem to be spotting," she said. I told her to call her doctor. She had. The doctor had told her to lie down and wait.

"Wait?" I asked. There was a little tremor that was beginning in my knee. "Wait for what?"

"I don't know." The voice of a Marion I had only rarely met. Scared.

"I'm coming home," I said.

I cooked us some veal chops, made a fruit salad. We settled in for the night, Marion on the couch with a throw and me in the rocker. Neither of us could read; we watched news, sitcoms, TV movies, anything we could find. Just after midnight, we slipped into our respective sides of the bed. We held hands. Marion stroked my thumb with hers. We tried to breathe.

I woke to Marion gasping. She was out of bed in a sweep that made our four-poster rattle. By the time I made it to the bathroom, the door was closed. It was locked. I could hear her crying. "Marion!" She didn't answer, later told me she couldn't, couldn't even unlock the door, could only sit and let all that we'd held like a prize, our sweetest prize yet, slip out of her.

"I'm sorry, Bun," she said when she finally came out.

She sobbed all night, that best, most brutal kind of crying, crying that remembers everything that ever hurt. Dreams were burned up in our bed that night.

Marion went in for a D&C the next afternoon. She stayed overnight, more drugged than I'd ever seen her. I stayed home from work the next day and the next. Our priest came to talk to us, a few of Marion's friends came by. One brought a boysenberry pie and advice about letting go: "It was probably all for the best," she said. "You never know what kind of problems you might have had later with the"—she paused on the word—"child." Another told us of her own miscarriage twenty years before. "You never forget," she said, eyes filling.

Marion's best friend, Ginny, even came by to meditate with her. From the bedroom I could hear them singing Compline, the last hymn of the day for Benedictine monks. Marion always ends her evening meditation this way. "A quiet night and a perfect end": that's always been one of my favorite lines, but that night I could not think of words further away from our life.

On the fifth day I left Marion on the couch—I could only rely on teachers assistants for so long—with stacks of books, the PBS guide for all-day viewing if that's what she wanted, and the phone plugged into a nearby jack. She'd put on lipstick that morning and had changed into clean sweats. She held me down longer than usual when I bent to kiss her, "Call me," she whispered. I promised to call every hour.

"Don't forget," she whispered. I thought it was still the effect of the anesthetic, the tube that had scraped her throat, made it sore.

I called at ten (she was reading the latest *Gourmet*), at eleven (listening to a radio call-in show—"mindless, but distracting," said Marion). At noon, a friend came over to fix lunch as arranged. Marion sounded okay, tired but okay. At one, she was settling down for a nap. I didn't call at two, wanting her to sleep. When I phoned at three, I didn't recognize the voice that answered. It was a male voice. "Are you her husband?" he asked. "You'd better come home. Your wife...I think she needs you."

He was standing in the entryway with his coat on when I got there, a young man, not more than twenty-five, good-looking, straight-looking, with shiny new shoes and a hockey nose. He introduced himself as Kevin. His hand was clammy when I shook it. "I was just demonstrating the suction feature," he said, gesturing down to his feet and a large, dark suitcase. "Kirby Vacuum Cleaners, sir," he said. "I don't know what happened, sir. One minute..." and then he got a panicky look on his face, as if he was seeing something again. He picked up the suitcase and was out the door, down the steps.

I hurried to find Marion. She wasn't in the living room. Or in the kitchen, although the light was on. I found her lying in our bed, lying flat without a pillow. She was under the bedspread, but not the sheets.

"I really blew it, Bun," she said.

The young salesman—this is the story she told me that evening after she'd apologized and cried and napped and cried—had rung the bell around 1:15. She remembered looking at the clock and noting the time. She told me—she smiled as she said this—that the only reason she could imagine the doorbell ringing in the middle of the afternoon was for flowers.

"Flowers?" I said.

"From you," she said.

I groaned.

"That's okay," she said.

The young man was selling vacuum cleaners. But more important than that, he said, he wanted to offer a service. He wanted to shampoo our carpet.

"I thought, what the hell? My life is a mess, let's clean up one little corner of it," Marion told me. "I thought it was a sign."

"Of what?" I asked.

"God's grace," said my wife. I didn't say anything, for fear I would laugh or cry.

"So I let him in, Bun. He seemed nice. He *was* nice. He wasn't the problem." She stopped, afraid of crying again; I was setting the TV trays we'd been eating all our meals on that week, but I stopped, sat down on the bed next to her.

"It was probably too soon to see anybody. From outside, you know," I said.

"His machine was the problem," said Marion. "At first it was okay. He didn't talk much. He went about his duty, just like he said: No hard sales pitch. Just service. He actually said that. But then, while the carpet was drying, he asked if he could come sit in the living room and chat with me a bit. I didn't know how to say 'no' after all the work he'd done. Just let me tell you about the Kirby, he said, as if he were talking about his dog or his best friend. Let me tell you about the Kirby. And then he sat down on the other end of the couch and he took out this long hose and he hooked it up to the unit, you know, the motor or whatever, and he's talking at the top of his voice about the Kirby's super suction capabilities, how it can clean out anything, anywhere, and I couldn't help it...the sound of his voice and the machine...I just couldn't stand it. I hated them so much. I hated everything." Marion looked in my face, at my left eye, which she still does when she wants to get through. "I screamed," she said.

I held her all night and she held me. Sometime just before the sun came up, I let myself think about the child. "I love you both," I had told Marion one week before. I didn't scream—Marion had screamed for both of us—but I did cry in that hour before dawn.

I must have been sitting here for some time, although I don't remember exactly choosing this chair, Marion's kitchen chair, the one with the view of the lilac bush. Little buds have appeared in the past few days; we've been monitoring them closely. Marion's an absolute maniac for lilacs.

I hear her come in. She sets a glass in the sink.

"Done," she announces, "though I've got to admit, this one wasn't quite up to par. Okay, okay, I know, Parker's repetitious, and he might not ever write as well as he did in *Rachel Wallace*," she says, looking at me, guessing at what I would normally say, since I'm half the fan she is. "But think about it, Bun, how could you spit out a novel like this every year and not have a dud or two?"

I nod, point to the lilac buds, which in the descending dark look like pussy willows. She comes up from behind. I can feel the warmth of her.

"Why didn't you remind me?" I ask, surprised that I sound bitter.

"I didn't need to, did I?" she says.

"Yes, but I went through most of the day without remembering."

"Is that so bad?" Marion asks. She drops down near me, her head a little below mine so she can see the lilacs-to-be. "Oh, quiet night," she says.

Sayonara

The apartment is exactly the way she remembers it, though a few prints are missing here and there. What has become of the Rousseau, the one they discovered they both owned, she wonders, as he follows her into the bedroom. Where is the couple in white moving across dark fields?

Other than this, all is the same. He's as compact as ever (short, she's called him in the ensuing years, "a midget really"), as dense when she hugs him, as swift in being able to whip off her sweater and press her to his ever-ready self.

"I thought you might never come back," he says.

She never planned to. He had driven her insane with his vagueness and hot-air ego, his expert aim as a lover. With him she'd felt like someone at an all-you-can-eat buffet, stuffed, but ready to be hungry all over again. "A banquet of pain," she thinks, congratulating herself that even in this decisive moment she still has her mind in tow, her observations at the ready. Laszlo secures her hips more certainly into his.

She has not seen him in four years.

What happened was this: Margo was driving home, having taken her son to the international airport far outside the city. He is her youngest, Sean, her special one. Her daughter, Heather, the less-favorite one—Margo is becoming more honest as her children grow up; they've forced her into such honesty—is away at university, in the same town as her father. Father and daughter recently reconnected after a long spell of absence and disaffection, Christmas cards only, so that now all seems settled between them.

I am alone now. This was the thought that greeted her in the airport parking lot as she turned the key in the old Honda. The car choked, shuddered, barely caught. Sean would be on the plane now, cruising the radio channels. Japan Airlines wouldn't carry anything he'd like. His musical tastes were eclectic (his word), bizarre (hers). Or maybe he was looking out the plane window, maybe he was trying to find her through the dark glass of the terminal. Had he wanted her to stay until takeoff? They hadn't discussed it. Should she go back and hang around? Would she even know when his plane had gone? What if his little porthole was on the other side, facing away from the terminal? It would be a waste then to go back. If only they'd discussed what he wanted.

She rubbed the inside of the windshield with the sleeve of her wool coat, knowing it wouldn't accomplish anything, then pulled out of the parking lot and eased onto the frontage road. That was when she knew where she was going.

In the bedroom, Laszlo runs his hand up her right arm, then down, a surprisingly warming gesture. "Should I ask for explanations?" he asks. She takes his hand, makes it do the same up and down her other arm, a kind of answer.

"How's work?" he says.

"A few commissions here and there."

"Ditto," he says.

She paints, he sculpts. The frayed life of the mostly unrecognized middle-aged artist. So all is really the same.

"Keep rubbing," she says.

Instead, he lifts both arms and peels off his sweater, that same dreary gray thing from years back. He's wearing a bright yellow T-shirt underneath. She doesn't remember it. He might have bought an article or two of clothing since they last undressed together.

"I heard you got married," he says.

"You heard right," she says. "I happen to be, in fact, still married."

He pulls her down to sit next to him, leans over her knees and begins rolling down her socks, a surprisingly arousing gesture.

Sean wanted her, and only her, to drive him to the airport. He could have asked his girlfriend, Gabrielle, or his best friend. "I want my good old mom," he insisted the week before. "Who else gets it? I mean, you know... really gets what this trip means to the whole of my life? Like who else remembers me and those origami cranes?"

"I remember a lot of crunched-up paper," she said, laughing. Sean's fascination with all things Japanese had been a matter of pride and some amusement since grammar school days.

"And that Noh play I tried to put on, when I was what? In grade seven? Even the teachers thought I was weird?" Sean's statements still curled into questions. He still said "you know" a lot. He was twenty-one, but still a kid.

They'd been talking about Gabrielle, how she wanted him to write her every day and how already he knew he would disappoint her. "Do you think that's fair?" he asked his mother, looking worried. He was one of those kids born with a serious face, clouded by conscience. Now he'd grown into it. He sat at the kitchen table in his swimming trunks and bare feet even though it was the dead of winter.

"Gabrielle needs to cut you some slack," she told him. "This is your year, Cookie."

"Cookie yourself," he said, smiling, but sliding away from an early endearment. They were quiet, adjusting to new, necessary distances.

"I even asked Heather what she thought."

"You're kidding," she said. It always surprised Margo when her two children came together on anything. They shared no turf. What they had in common was her as a mother, and that was mostly, agonizingly, a source of conflict for all of them.

Or had been. It was all shifting lately. She didn't mind if nothing ever changed in her life again, but there it was: every day something new. Ron, her husband, thought her resentment of change was an early sign of menopause. Ron attributed much of what she said and felt to hormones. Hers, not his.

Heather had played older sister to the hilt apparently. Had advised Sean to be clear about what he needed this year. "Tell Gabrielle what *she* can gain, too, from this time apart, that's what she told me," Sean said.

"Sane advice," Margo agreed.

"Yeah, but what I really need is some totally insane advice from my ma," he said and came up from behind and grabbed her in a sumo-wrestler hug.

"Then don't go. Let those Japanese businessmen learn English from some other Canadian kid," she said, holding still, not turning around. There was a second where they both realized she might not be joking. Then laughter. Funny, Mom.

They had travelled together many times. Not to Europe, no grand global expeditions like the one he was about to make to Japan, but runs to Boston and D.C. and Freeport. One summer they'd camped on Prince Edward Island. And the Christmas Sean was eleven they'd driven all the way to Florida. Heather had stayed behind with a friend and her family so Margo and Sean had each other to themselves for once. They stayed three days, barely sleeping, hitting one Disney attraction after another, then drove the whole way back in as many days, with Margo sleeping an hour at a stretch in rest areas along the highway. It was too cold to park longer than that. When she thinks back to that trip she shudders with remembered cold and the sense of having pulled off something foolhardy. Sean said it was his best time ever.

Her socks are off. The wood floor is cold. "Here," Laszlo says, and lifts both her feet, forcing her to lean back. Her elbows catch her; it's too soon to go completely supine. He strokes her feet, not quite a massage, not quite the brisk, frictional rubdown she used to give the kids when they came in with soggy boots and frozen toes.

And then his hands are drawing down her leggings, drawing down his own pants, and her head hits something solid. There is no pillow behind her. She is perfectly flat. "I can't believe this," he says and lowers himself onto her. He pulls the blanket up and over. "I can't believe how hard you can still make me," he says and finds her, the opening to her, with an ease so extreme, she actually gasps.

Sean was quiet on the drive to the airport, mainly saying yes and no. Margo told him about a story she'd just read in the business section of the newspaper about the rash of Japanese noodle shops. "Everyone eats noodles everywhere all the time. The way we eat hamburgers. It's amazing. You've got to write and tell me what they're like. I'm sure you'll be eating a lot of noodles. In between teaching and studying and traveling and everything. Maybe you can Air Express me some." Talking, talking.

She saw him nod as they passed under a yellow highway lamp. "You know I love noodles." He watched the road in front of them as he said this, seemed to be calculating something to himself. How much of her bravura chatter to let in perhaps. How much of himself to let out. He'd told her a few days before, "I'm going to miss you so much I can't even think about it."

This trip had been long in the talking and planning. (Trip wasn't the right word, she kept correcting herself in the days before his departure; trips usually involve a return ticket.) Even Ron had been part of the planning, one of the rare times he'd ventured into the dreams of her children.

After Sean signed on with the language institute in Kyoto, they took him out for sushi. Sean sat between Ron and Margo at the bar, Margo watching as the men, her two men, wrestled with the snug bundles of seaweed-wrapped rice. She saw flashes of chartreuse avocado, smelled dusty ginger. A careful person at heart—even her most revolutionary canvasses possessed a certain order—she had ordered chicken teriyaki.

"Try some sushi, Mom, you'll like it."

"Really, hon. It's kind of like guacamole goes Tokyo."

"Is that like *Gidget Goes Hawaiian?*" she asked, but stuck to her order.

The men sat, dark head, fair head, in semi-profile. Even their chopsticks were poised at the same angle, a rare alignment. Not to be outdone in his knowledge of Japan, Ron was telling Sean about *kaizen*. "It literally means continuous improvement." Their chopsticks were going like crazy: grabbing, snatching, sometimes missing. "The Japanese have it way over us, I'll tell you," said Ron. "And talk about educational standards."

Still, it was hard to be comfortable around the two of them. Something else could so quickly happen. A tone in someone's voice could be interpreted as a put-down. They had come to her often during the few years they'd lived under one roof, both of them, complaining, "He put me down." It was, she'd come to believe, the worst experience a man might have at the hands of another man.

To give him credit, Ron had tried, in that dogged way he tried at most things. But when he'd shown up in her son's seventeenth year, he'd been like a general issuing orders after the battle. She'd done her best, Margo tried telling her new husband, once yelling, "You try being a goddamned single mother!"

As headmaster at a boy's school, Ron's human currency was consequences. (Consequences, Margo believed, believed silently, was just a nineties word for reward and punishment.) "Action equals consequence," Ron liked to say. "Not always bad ones," he would add. "Just give me one example, if you can, of one thing that any person does that does not lead to something else. Can you? I mean, name one."

There will be consequences for this. She hadn't planned for this. She had actually entertained the possibility, as she drove the miles of frozen, familiar streets to his apartment, that she wouldn't see him at all. Would turn away from his door at the last second. Not stay long enough to feel the buzzer ring straight through and up her arm as she pressed it. Perhaps a woman would be there, perhaps a woman would be *living* there, perhaps there would be a child. Much can happen in four years. She'd met another man, after all. She'd even married him.

Laszlo is good at this. Good at her. He breathes into the side of her hair and then he whispers, *oh my god*. He is out of control with her again, the only way she ever loved him. And then he is apologizing with his lips for his haste, he is sliding down her body, sliding his tongue round and round that space small as a *centime* and she is doing what she never planned to do.

"I've missed you," she says. "Apparently." Trying to laugh, trying not to cry. The arches of her feet, the palms of her hands, every part of her has been blessed and released.

"I know," he says, "oh, dear heart, I know."

When they broke up the first time she'd been like a sick person. Her eyes burned, her legs wobbled. She wanted to throw up ten times a day. Laszlo was her flu.

Of course, life went on. It always went on if you were a mother. There were two teenagers to contend with. Heather was in love with some punker that summer, sat around the house listening to the guy's pirated tapes, and Sean was into making kites out of tissue paper and balsa wood. The place smelled of epoxy, throbbed with bad music, when all she wanted was to be alone, wanted the freedom to stare at the wall, to cry in the shower, to heal herself with her own hand, one orgasm after another, without some kid calling, Mom, you all right? Mom?

So it was true. Muscles, nerves, cells even, could gather together for something, for someone, they wanted so much that they would not let go. Laszlo was the first man to give Margo exactly what she wanted, not an approximation of it. She tried not to think about the other woman—he admitted there was someone else—or was it *women*? He was vague with singular and plural. And so specific with her.

"This...how does this feel?"

"Can you feel the pressure there?"

"I can feel your muscles twinging. Right...against...my...balls."

"You're killing me. I'll never be the same."

He was, Laszlo told her occasionally, equally hooked.

So when he came back after that summer, she asked only that he include her in whatever life he needed to fashion for himself. He was back. She could live with anything else.

He is at her temple, breathing with relief. Gladness even.

"I put Sean on a plane tonight," she says.

"Sayonara," Laszlo murmurs and anchors his cheek against her shoulder so that she can't sit up, can't begin searching for her bra, can only lie next to him and breathe into that terrible, beautiful word. She has betrayed her husband in less than fifteen minutes. Less time than it takes to ride the wretched exercycle at the gym, less time than it takes to gesso the smallest canvas. Far less time than it would ever take to explain all the possible causes, reasons and motivations. And, God forbid, discuss the consequences.

"I always thought," says Laszlo, not moving an inch away, "sayonara meant goodbye *and* hello."

She lies still, trying to figure out what he's telling her.

"He always comes back," says Laszlo.

In their second summer together, Sean, just sixteen, landed a job working construction. Margo worried about him in the first weeks. Worried he'd fall off a ladder, drive a nail through his thumb, get swallowed in a cement mixer. "He'll be fine," Laszlo kept saying. "We all survive our first jobs." And he told her about his first one repairing roofs. He'd worked with a couple of older men, real craftsmen, but borderline alcoholics. In the morning, the men supervised him carefully, even kindly. "Don't get overly cocky," they warned him. But by the afternoon, they themselves grew cocky, egos lubricated by a lunch that always included a six-pack each.

"It wasn't how much they drank, but how it affected them," he'd told her.

Margo knew all about alcoholism; her first husband, Heather's father, had had a problem holding his liquor and, consequently, jobs, friends and anything else that mattered. Sean's dad hadn't been much better. No booze, but he'd had a love affair with their credit cards. Men always seemed to overdo it in one arena or another. This realization had come to her only in midlife and armed her only slightly in the world of men.

The afternoon the phone rang was the hottest so far in that mild summer. A mighty heat was pumping everywhere, even off the dark green walls of her bedroom. Sean was at work, Heather at a class. They were meeting at her place for a change.

"I've only got half an hour," Laszlo said at the door. Something to do with his live-in girlfriend. His shirt was off by the time he crossed the living room. It was too hot for clothes, too hot for anything elaborate. He was already inside her when the phone rang.

"Leave it," she ordered.

"Better get it," he said on the fifth ring, and she reached behind her to the nightstand, willed by him, as she often was, to do something part of her wanted to refuse.

"Sean" was the only word she understood. And that there was a need to be afraid.

It turned out the person on the other end was speaking another language. Hungarian, Laszlo told her, as he drove to the hospital. His father was Hungarian. "I understand more than I can speak," he said.

He'd gotten her dressed. She remembered looking down at her khaki shorts and not-quite-clean tank top as he rushed through yellow lights going red, red lights going green, and wondered how she'd come to be wearing this particular outfit.

Sean had been moved from the emergency room to intensive care shortly before they arrived. They got this information from the ER clerk. No one seemed to know more. In those first long minutes when she fought to get her bearings, her wits, they tried flagging down ER doctors, ER nurses, anyone, finally, who could tell them what had happened.

In the end, Laszlo was the one who pieced it together, hearing a strange language spoken by two workmen standing at the other end of the hospital corridor. They were sweating, seemed excited. "Excuse me?" he said, crossing to them.

Josef and Tomas were "very sorry, very sorry." Sean had fallen— "Boom!" recounted Tomas with tears in his eyes—from a third-storey scaffold while installing a new window. Her son had been wearing a hard hat, but no safety belt. He'd been counting on his own good balance.

They didn't expect him to live. No one during those next days actually came out and said this, but he was in a coma and that was not good. The more days he stayed in that stillness so unlike sleep, the less likely he would ever regain consciousness.

"Is he strong?" one doctor asked Margo. "Does he have a strong constitution? You know, a strong will?" When Margo nodded (she'd found it hard, very hard, to speak much during those days), he only said, "Okay."

She sat by his bed for four days and a good part of a fifth. She didn't read, didn't even look out the window that had a nearly aerial view of the city. It seemed a sin, that view, that week.

Once Laszlo picked her up and took her to his apartment for a shower, not worrying for once about his girlfriend. Sean's accident, he told Margo, had made him get honest with the other woman in a way he'd been avoiding.

"I know where my loyalties are now," he said. He held her after the shower, brushed her hair.

"I don't know if I can live without him," she told him. He slowed his strokes, barely touching her scalp with the hairbrush.

Heather came every day after her classes, stayed until visiting hours ended, although she and her half-brother had been engaged in one of their cold wars at the time. He had asked to borrow one of her two cameras for a backpacking trip and she'd refused.

"Mom, face it, she's just not like us. She's got a stone in here." Sean had thumped his chest. This was the week before. Before all this sitting. Now as she watched her daughter watch her son, she wanted to ask, "Why couldn't you just have given the guy your goddamn camera?"

Heather's brown hair was incredibly, not attractively, long that summer. She wore it braided in two long switches and she played obsessively with the uneven ends. With one hand, she twirled; with the other, she kept an equally obsessive grip on her brother's hand, which she retrieved each afternoon from under the tight hospital bedding.

"Mother, hold his other hand, why don't you?" she asked one afternoon, and looked over at Margo with such incomprehension that Margo put her hand on her son's. She felt more tubing and tape than skin, could barely bring herself to touch him. Still, she held her hand there as long as Heather was in the room.

At the end of her watch, Heather disengaged her hand from Sean's. "Call me if..." she said. When the door closed behind her, Margo tried to cry. But the tears, like her speech, were stuck in some bricked-over place.

The first sign was flexing in the middle finger of his left hand— the one Heather had gripped for five days—"like you were playing air guitar," Margo told her son a few days later. The doctors now said they had assumed all along he would pull out of it.

About a week later, when Sean was in a nearby rehabilitation centre, it all came unstuck. Shock, grief, fear—all delayed—took up residence in her chest. Her ribs ached from the flood. She wondered what was wrong with her.

On the second day of feeling like this, she called Laszlo. He couldn't come over tonight, what about tomorrow? No, wait, tomorrow wasn't so good either. Maybe they'd better hold off and rendezvous next week.

"I'm not doing all that great," she told him.

He got beeped. "I'll call you back," he said and didn't.

Sean came home a week later, terribly thin. Margo fed him elaborate meals, more elaborate snacks. It was just the two of them, except for the few times Heather came to pick up her things. She was moving in with a girlfriend for the fall semester. "It'll be easier on everyone this way," she said, and Margo didn't argue.

One night when Heather was there, Margo told Sean how his sister had clutched his hand hour after hour. "She cast a spell on you, a good spell," she told Sean.

"It was what I'd do for anyone," Heather informed them.

Eventually Laszlo called. Eventually they started up again. Sex—good, great, best sex—with some food after.

"This is damn good," he said one of those times, leaning against the kitchen counter. He was frying garlic in olive oil. A smoky, sweet cloud hung over them. It was three in the morning.

"The garlic?" she asked.

"You know what I mean," he said.

Sean held onto the elbow of her coat when they hugged goodbye at the airport. "Keep Gabrielle in line, okay?" he said. "Reassure her and stuff? She's so insecure."

Margo promised, but she knew already they wouldn't last six months. Gabrielle didn't have that kind of bravery. You have to be brave to love, or you have to act brave, this is what she was thinking as her cheek grazed the shoulder of her son's coat.

She didn't have to be brave with Ron. Theirs was a getting-through kind of love. Basically goodwilled, useful at times, steadying, for her anyway, after a lifetime of strenuous, dangerous loving. Marriage for a safe middle age.

"Give Sean my best," Ron had told her on the phone as she was leaving the house for the airport. "Make sure he understands it might be pretty tough in the beginning, the cultural adjustment and all." Then added, "You're going to be okay, aren't you?"

"I think so," she said.

"Drive carefully," he said. "Winter roads."

Sean didn't cry, not exactly, as he walked away, trying to wave while he adjusted his carry-on. But his eyes were wide and the gesture of his hand was small. "I love you," he mouthed as he turned the "Passengers Only" corner. By the time she realized what he'd said, she was waving at his bag.

"I need to go home," she says.

"Goodbye again," he says.

"I miss my son," she says, not making it through the last word because what she really wants to say is *I miss my family* and because she has just imagined Sean on the plane, moving miles per minute in that other direction—away. Laszlo holds her until she can inhale without the breath catching in her throat and then he helps her find the parts of her former self: socks, bra, belt. He re-layers her for her return.

At the door he kisses her. "Any time, any year," he says. Then he closes the door behind her, not waiting for her to leave. She remembers the sound of that door, the wood at her heels, the way it felt to step out, not to be able to fall back into *anything*, to walk away not knowing when and if she would come back. One time it had been the last. One time she had survived what came next.

She stands on the top step, contemplating the one below it.

Walking the Dog

I have known couples who rarely spoke to each other, but each spoke to their dog. The dog became a link across the silence, became a place to deposit messages from the other side, from the far sides of a marriage.

By the time Candace and Parker reached me—this was toward the end of September, the end of our good weather, the end of my second terrible summer—they were talking to Lalapalooza and rarely speaking to each other. They'd been driving cross-country since June, from L.A. to Burlington, looking for someplace new to settle. I was their last stop, Montreal. They weren't considering settling here; it was to be more of a visit than a scouting expedition. We hadn't seen each other since I'd moved away with my husband and son six years before.

"That's a brave undertaking," I told them, "just hitting the road in a van like that. And then trying to be so open to every new place. And, of course, at the same time you're trying to be discerning. You're trying to weigh all the pros and cons of a place. What did you think of Burlington, by the way?"

We were sitting in my small living room after we'd lugged all their stuff up to my second-floor flat. Their stuff included Lalapalooza's dog bed and dog toys, three stuffed animals that were either bears or cats or rabbits. I couldn't tell. I found myself talking a lot and talking very fast. We'd hardly written during these past six years.

"It's been tough, hasn't it, Lala, darling?" crooned Candace and ran her hand between his ears. She did this back and forth several times so Lala's chestnut hair stood on end.

I'm not overly fond of dogs, but I'll grant that Lala is a specimen. He has a stately turn to his head, a face like you see often among the British aristocracy—long cheeks and world-weary eyes.

"It hasn't been *that* bad, has it, Lala? The trip's only been as tough as we've made it," Parker said. "I thought Burlington was neat. But ask Candace. She had a radically different experience." He looked at Candace and put his hand down on the floor. The dog looked at Candace, kept looking back at her, until he reached Parker's upturned palm, which he began to lick. It was a slobbery lick; I heard the saliva in it.

"Mommy thought Burlington was like the rest of Vermont, didn't she, sweet thing? Green and boring," said Candace and put her hand out. Lala looked back at Parker and trotted the four feet to his mistress. I put my hands under my seat.

Lala licked the tips of Candace's fingers—"Salt from potato chips," she explained to me. And then the auburn creature bent his front legs, lowered his weight, shifted, and there he was: our centrepiece.

"Better than flowers," I said.

"Huh?" said Candace.

"I'll get us something to eat," said Parker and disappeared into my kitchen.

"So, sweetie, how are you coping? Have you talked to your sister lately? Of course you haven't. How dumb of me. I'm sorry, it's just we've been driving so much, so many stupid hours in the van and if you only knew what the Midwest is like, it's absolutely deadening. My brain is on tilt. How are you? Really?"

I looked at Candace and saw the woman I remembered: the mighty mane of red hair, the dancer's back, the angled front tooth that slightly, charmingly, nudged the other one out. She was fifty, but still a daredevil beauty.

"I remember Nebraska," I said. I could give her the *Reader's Digest* version of my state of heart, the one I'd edited down to a dry-eyed paragraph. But it was too early to get into her questions, my tragedies.

We had hours to go. "Home, home on the range and all that. I remember we couldn't find cheddar cheese. Only good ol' American. Yellow plastic processed shit."

"No Kraft slices in your kitchen," said Parker, appearing with a tray—the lacquered one from Hong Kong my parents had just sent, the one I hadn't even used yet—now piled high with a plate of crackers, three glasses, a bottle of wine I didn't recognize, and the hunk of Friulano I'd planned to use in tonight's Alfredo sauce.

"Hope I haven't trespassed any boundaries," said Parker as he put the magazines from the coffee table onto the floor to make room for the tray. "I've got a bit of hypoglycemia, don't I, Lala? If I don't *manger* every few hours, I'm a shaky son of a gun."

"I had no idea how serious it was until we flew to Paris last year," Candace said. "We had, I don't know, some kind of problem, some delay at de Gaulle and it was another hour before we got off the plane. Parker hadn't eaten for seven hours and he was like a zombie by then and for another day he was still quite out of it. It freaked me completely. Ever since then we don't take any chances, do we, Lala?"

Lala was asleep at our feet. He was snoring, a wet sound. Maybe everything about dogs is wet, I thought. Maybe they're just one large mucous membrane.

"Are you crying a lot?" Parker asked me through the cheese in his mouth. "You know, to cleanse and everything? It's very important to empty ourselves out after a loss. When my dad died I stayed in bed and cried for four days straight."

"Yes, I'm crying," I said and reached for the Friulano. Maybe we'd go out to dinner.

Candace put her hand on mine. "Let yourself grieve," she said. "You have a lot to grieve for. Two big losses in one year. Whewww!" As she said "Whewww!" Lala raised his head and looked at me. Blinked once, then lay his head back down, the full length of his neck flat to the floorboards. He closed his eyes.

"It's more like three losses," I began to say. "Sometimes I think I miss Sue nearly…"

"Got any fruit?" asked Parker, but he was already on his way to the kitchen.

"I heard she, Sue, has had a rough time of it. You know, a lot of guilt and all," said Candace. Lala opened his eyes, nothing else moving, and looked at me.

"Lala just gave me the most interesting look," I said.

"Great depths of compassion," said Candace. "A psychic in Minneapolis told us Lala is going to come back as light in his next incarnation."

"Light?" I looked down at the now-snoring dog.

"His energy's been refined over the course of many lifetimes. It doesn't surprise me." Candace leaned down to stroke Lala's flank.

We observed a few moments of quiet, pondering Lala's future non-dog life. I tried to imagine Lala as light, as a great, leaping trapezoid of light, light with its tongue hanging out, light with the unmistakable whiff of dog. Candace probably saw a sweet, heavenly blur, not so much a defined beam of brightness, but a presence, an aura. I smiled. To myself, I thought, but Lala looked up at me again, blinked, then stood up, heaving his considerable hulk first to his back legs, then to his front. He leaned toward me, put his nose against my knee.

"He wants to go for a walk," said Candace. "With all this driving, we haven't been getting our full quota of walks, have we, darling?"

"I'll take him," I said, surprising myself and apparently Candace. She looked at me, trying to read my emotional state.

"Well, if…" she said.

"I've been in the house all day," I told her, talking too fast again. "This will give you guys a chance to unwind, catch your breath. Lala can see the neighborhood." I stood up, all business.

I could feel the temperature dropping outside, even through two layers of glass. As I passed the kitchen, I saw Parker. He was standing at the counter, his nose in one of those long baguette bags. I remembered there was just a stump of a loaf left. He looked up, flushed, started rolling the bag closed as if it were a sleeping bag. The noise of paper made it difficult to hear him. He'd begun talking as soon as he'd seen me. He motioned me to come into the room.

"See the thing is, I went bonkers over Burlington. Sounds like a song, huh? Did I tell you I used to live there, well, near there? Back in the '60s, one of those back-to-nature things. It worked for a while, then

I got fed up with the rednecks and moved to L.A. Now I'm fed up with the weirdos there."

Up close, I noticed Parker had crumbs on one cheek. He must have eaten the rest of the bread. And up close, I saw how short he was. Our eyes were level and I'm only five-three. Amazing the things we forget about people.

He put his hand on my shoulder. "I even tried to convince her how great it would be to live so close to you. Talk to her, will you? We fought all the way up here. She thinks Vermont's not sophisticated enough. But I keep telling her if we go with sophistication, we'll end up back with all the craziness we're trying to get away from: crime, smog, high prices, people on drugs, people on the streets. You should see Santa Monica these days. You trip over homeless people on every street. Literally trip over them. It's the damn climate. If the weather was worse, we wouldn't have half this trouble."

Lala padded into the kitchen, went for the back of my knees this time, a forceful nudge. He carried a plaid leash in his mouth. The metal hook trailed behind him, clicking on the linoleum like tap shoes. Candace must have given it to him.

"I'm walking the dog," I told Parker, kissed him on the cheek without crumbs, and went to get my jacket. "Relax, eat, listen to some music," I called as I went down the stairs. No one answered. Parker was still in the kitchen; Candace still in the living room apparently.

I'd misjudged the temperature outside. It was warmer than it looked from inside. The wind that was tossing the trees felt like it came from the south. Still, there was caution in it. I knew not to get too comfortable. Just around the corner a sudden cold front might move in.

Lala paused at the end of the front sidewalk, sniffed, blinked a few times rapidly, then turned right and took off, cantering like a pony. It was a light, effortless pace. I'd expected balance-defying tugs, unpredictable lurches. I'd never found walking dogs to be easy, or particularly fun. My sister Sue's dog once jerked so hard I landed face down on cement. But in that moment upstairs, with the opportunity for departure offered, I'd lunged at the chance. Please, let me walk him.

Now Lala was leading the way; all I had to do was keep a reasonable grip on the leash and follow. It was about five o'clock; the remaining light was being blotted by charcoal clouds. We'd give this a half-hour, then turn back. *Then* I'd deal with dinner. Without the Friulano—Parker and Candace had turned the hefty wedge into a slender triangle—I'd have to come up with some other sauce. I had crushed peppers, maybe just enough olive oil.

We turned a corner and the surprise was there—the bitterness I knew lay hidden at the centre of this mild September wind. It shocked us both. Lala's ears went back, the little bell around his neck clanged, a flat, protesting sound. I gasped, instinctively hunched my shoulders, blinked against the assault of fast-moving, freezing air. They teared, my eyes, and as if reminded of what they really wanted to do, what they wanted to do day and night in this cruelest of summers, they began to weep. We trotted along the cold sidewalks and I cried. Lala was discreet, did not look back, just kept going.

We were now a good mile from the house, on a street I didn't know. The trees were dancing all around us, maples, oaks, elms. We passed some madly swaying ferns with magenta stamens huge as bottle brushes. We were in the tropics, only it was Montreal and it was cold and I was crying.

We were trotting past an open lot, an open lawn with a weeping willow and lilac bushes, when Lala's legs stopped moving; his hindquarters skidded to a stop. He sniffed the wind, then veered right. He was taking me across the lawn. I began to balk, but he tugged— gently; it was not an intrusive, come-on-you-lazy-carcass-of-a-human tug, the kind I've seen so many dogs inflict on their owners. We tripped lightly across the lawn that did not belong to anyone I knew. Lala circled us behind the willow. Some of the fronds hung so low, they brushed the top of my head.

Behind the tree, on the leafy, crunchy lawn sat an old tire. It was gray with weather, its tread erased by a million miles. That tire made me think of my parent's first house, of long, sweet summers and it made me think of my sister, the one person I did not want to think about. Lala sat by the tire and tugged me down to his level. I sat on the tire's cracked edge and looked up at the house. The windows were dark. There weren't even curtains in some. Lala's tail twitched, kicking up a few leaves. He looked out toward the street, keeping guard, letting me have my private moment.

When we were little, my sister and I would squeeze our skinny legs through the hole of a tire like this, sit face-to-face and pump for all we were worth to get the thing moving. Once—as we were arcing to our highest, most thrilling point—the rope snapped. We flew, the tire with us, onto the lawn where we lay screaming for a long time, long after the shock of impact, long after the fear had passed. We liked the sound of all that drama coming from just us.

Watching Lala's tail, I realized I wasn't crying any more. It happened like this: great bursts of wailing, then quiet. I almost hated the quiet more. It was when my mind took over, began building its own little stories and reasons. My mind was an escape artist. The crying was pure, like light streaming in and out.

Two summers ago, my husband decided to move back to the West Coast. He'd been in love with my younger sister, Sue, for years, absolutely years. David told me this while he was holding me. He meant no harm, he said. Only now it was his turn to be happy. Their turn. Sue had been every bit as miserable as he, he told me. We tried not to love each other, he said. God, we tried.

This summer, our son, who is eleven, went west, too. "I don't have that many friends in Montreal, Mom, and I miss Dad." Evan's voice had broken over the word "Dad" all that long winter as we tried to make a life built for three fit two. It would be fine with Aunt Sue, he reassured me. "She loves me a lot. Not like you, but it will be okay."

They were doing okay, Evan continued to reassure me when he called every Sunday. They'd gone camping this summer, his first time. They'd signed him up for soccer this fall, Little League in the spring. "Are you okay, Mom?" he asked me each time before saying goodbye. I knew this was his most anxious, unfavorite moment of the week. I tried to make it easy for him, but lately, I had to admit, I'd put less effort into it. The more cheerful I was on the phone, the more I cried after.

I thought of Parker and Candace trekking across the country searching for someplace that felt right, someplace with a good vibe and wondered if I should do that. I would have to change my idea of home. I knew this.

I let my weight fall back into the centre of the tire. Lala edged closer, sat on my feet. His weight and warmth held my feet down; they felt like flying up into the air and Lala held them down. I cried some more and then I ran out of Kleenex and Lala got off my feet and we walked home. The sky was lighter than when we'd left, an unexpected clearing before dark.

I heard the blender when I opened the front door. I barely recognized the sound. Since "the boys," as I'd taken to calling my husband and son, had left, I'd been living mostly on cans of refried beans and tortilla chips. Lala scrambled up the stairs, the leash slapping each step.

"Lalapalooza! Where have you been? Oh, we missed you! Oh, sweetie, your nose is so cold," I heard Candace trill.

I walked into the living room and there was Candace in a lace bra and no panties. Her clothes, the black leggings and long maroon tunic she'd arrived in, were in a puddle by the fireplace. Someone had started a fire. The small, Oriental carpet that was normally under the coffee table had been dragged dangerously near the fireguard.

"We made up!" said Candace, reaching for her leggings and watching my eyes moving among my furniture, trying to piece the last hour together. "Thank God for sex. It solves absolutely everything. Well, most things. We've decided to go back to L.A. and have a good think. Re-read our journals—it's so easy to just remember the little icky niggling things about a place. And besides, Parker doesn't want to make any big moves without consulting his therapist."

Lala was watching from the doorway. He looked exhausted. I followed him down the hall to the kitchen where Parker was now making a lot of noise; something was grinding that should have been whirring.

"*Salut!*" he greeted me. "How do you like my French? I think I put the blade in wrong. I was just whipping up a little hummus—hope you don't mind. There was a can of garbanzos in your cabinet and some oil."

"They were for the salad I was planning on making," I said.

"Oh," said Parker. "Well, no harm done. Hummus is pretty yummy stuff."

"I don't like hummus," I said. "And besides, I don't have any pita."

"We'll go to the store," he said. "They'll take American money, won't they?"

"The stores are closed," I said.

"It's only six," he said, looking horrified.

"This is Quebec," I told him. "It's Sunday. Grocery stores close at five."

"Ahh, old religious constrictions, huh?" he said. "It's amazing the things that are still done, the crimes still committed in the name of religion. Never on Sunday, oh, no, no, no."

Parker peered into the bottom of the blender, tried poking it with a salad tong. "Seems to be stuck," he said. Lala, who'd been lying under the kitchen table, began to whine. Candace came to the doorway. She was wearing clothes.

"Is Daddy making a mess again?" she asked the dog. "In the last place we stayed, you know, with our friends in Burlington, Parker broke the food processor. We're going to have to mail them a new one when we get the chance," she told me. Then to Lala, "Isn't that true, sweetie?"

I looked down at Lala and Lala looked up at me. "Excuse me," I said. I went down the hall to my room, partly closed the door, groped my way to the window and the rocker that sat near it. I didn't want to turn any lights on. I heard Parker whirring, then grinding the blender some more, then music from the living room, some Beatles Candace had found.

I rocked for awhile, wondering when I'd have the courage to go back out there. I thought of the old tire and the curtainless windows in the big house. I thought about the weather, how cold it would soon be and how dark. I thought of my sister, my son, my husband. About how much you can miss people who are still alive. I wondered again about buying a van, about hitting the road.

I felt it before I heard it. The solid, relaxed weight of a dog on my feet.

About the Author

Denise Roig moved to Montreal from Los Angeles in 1989 when her twelve-year-old daughter, Ariel, convinced her they should run away so Ariel could join the circus. Ariel went to study with Montreal's Cirque du Soleil and Denise has been living in Montreal ever since.

A Quiet Night and a Perfect End is Roig's first published collection of short stories, but she has been writing professionally for twenty years, specializing in corporate magazine writing. She has taught magazine writing and editing at Concordia University and recently developed a program for teaching story writing to elementary schoolchildren. A former Montreal *Gazette* columnist, she is a book reviewer for CBC's "Home Run" program, a co-organizer of the Urban Wanderers Reading Series (with husband Raymond Beauchemin), co-editor of Hochelaga Press' *The Urban Wanderers Reader* and past fiction editor of *Index*.